Sahnedra

THE VAMPIRE CHRONICLES

DAREN LESTER

BALBOA.
PRESS

A DIVISION OF HAY HOUSE

Balboa Press books may be ordered through booksellers or by contacting:

Balboa Press
A Division of Hay House
1663 Liberty Drive
Bloomington, IN 47403
www.balboapress.com
1 (877) 407-4847

Print information available on the last page.

ISBN: 978-1-5043-4106-6 (sc)
ISBN: 978-1-5043-4107-3 (e)

Balboa Press rev. date: 09/25/2015

CHAPTER 1

And so it begins.

In 1492, I had become reborn during the time that the Renaissance was still taking place and spreading like wildfire all over Europe. It was an exciting time; a time where many local plagues and diseases would strike various parts of the world like judgments from God and yet it was also a time of renewal and hope.

Many of us had actually begun to look forward to a world full of opportunities and wealth and to a time when many of those that were being persecuted for their religious beliefs had started trusting that things would change and become better and tolerance would begin to take hold in Eurasia for a true period of peace and prosperity for all.

As with any peace, there's always someone or some group of religious nuts that seem happy to go about destroying everything and bringing about untold suffering to the innocent around them. And so it was in 1492. Religious persecutions and wars seemed to spring up over and over again all over Europe and the Middle East and disease seemed to come oftentimes as a result of these wars due to the rotting corpses that were lying all over the fields of Europe. And the rest of the world had a lack of manpower to truly bury all of them in a timely manner.

And so is my tale. A tale of happiness and yet a darkening sorrow that would soon fill my life. I had times of joy and laughter and yes, there were times of heartache and sorrow, but the times I enjoy remembering the most are the good times with my mother, father and my two younger sisters.

I was born in 1474 in the small, yet lovely village of Satu Mare which has a long and proud history of its own. It was founded around 1213 or at least that is the given time that it was publicly acknowledged as a village by outsiders. I called it home. It was a place where one would like to raise a family, have a small home and yes, even a chicken or two. My little home was right in the middle of Europe where all the travelers from the East and the West would journey through to bring their goods from Western Europe to the Asian world and vice versa.

But, along with that as anyone knows as goods are transported from one side of the world to the other, oftentimes there are unintended consequences that come with these trading caravans. Along with the goods come people, animals, disease, blight and oftentimes refugees from villagers being misplaced due to war in some far off distant land that is filled with hunger and disease that soon leaks into the local population.

Such as it was for my small village. A small village that was surrounded by what always seemed to be a bigger village or nation or empire that seemed to spread from the north, south, east or west. And there we were. My small family and I dealing with life in whatever comes. Our faith had made us so strong that we could overcome anything. Our small country is now bordered by what is known as Ukraine, Serbia, Bulgaria, Hungary, Moldova and the Black Sea. And if you know your history, then you know we were in the middle of a lot of empires seeking to move out and upward all of the time.

But even though the powers of the world came and went as they are still doing today, my family survived in relative peace and prosperity. I was born into wealth and privilege and lived as a young girl in a private estate or as many today would call it, a castle. No, it may not have been a fortress as some may envision it, but it was a castle no less. It was my home where balls were held and parties were thrown. Townspeople would come and request help with an issue or try to settle a dispute.

Many young and beautiful women would come and ask my Father for permission to be married and then the young man would have to come and present his intentions for the young lady before my Father and the families of the intended joining. And then and only then could the local priest perform the wedding ceremony with the blessings of the local bishop and the ruling duke of the region who was my Father.

I was so proud to be the child of a ruling duke. A duke that not only ruled fairly and justly, but also was always looking out for what was best for his people and yes, even more his own children and family.

My Father was a loving man and loved his small country that God had entrusted to his care. I remember him telling me that he loved the rolling green hills and how the sun came up over the mountains in the morning and yes, even the taste of the first snowflake to fall from the sky that he could catch upon his tongue during the start of the cold winter season.

I remember him looking out over the land and just stare into the distance at all of the small huts on the sides of the hills that had just seemed to spread out and go on as if they would never end. Our village may have been small, but to us it was a bit of heaven.

My Father was named Dargon and my dear Mother was named Vinician and my two younger sisters were Myra and Vilian. This was my family in a nutshell. A small, yet happy family that did everything together when we could as long as the affairs of state business did not demand the time of my Father or Mother which seemed to be almost never-ending. The only time my parents had made an exception to the rule of state first was on our birthdays or any and all religious holidays and during Mass. My parents were very devout and religious people and I believe that is why I am so focused today because my sisters and I were raised to plan and prepare for almost any future event. My Father and Mother were grooming us to rule in their stead if anything should happen to them. We had some of the most learned scholars in our area and they drilled our minds until we would be able to quote what seemed like anything from the Bible to Gamaliel. At the time, it was long, wearisome work but now I look upon it and I wish I could go back to my small village of Satu Mare and relive the good old days.

The days when there were no computers, cell phones, DNA scans and far less pollution in the air, water and food supply. In the days of my youth, I could run and drink from a spring of water, eat a fish from a pond that was freshly caught and all this without fear of a disease or sickness from having taken it out of a local fishery. Yes, things were much different back in my day. The days before the darkness consumed me and almost destroyed my entire village.

The darkness that would have claimed all that it could devour and there was no mercy for the aged, youth or the innocent. We had no cures for it, no vaccines and no defense to repel such an invader and sadly, it came to us with a small group of innocent victims themselves. A small band of refugees fleeing the terror of the Ottoman Empire. For years, I hated them and would have sought to destroy them if I could have found any of them still alive, but sadly and mercifully the darkness consumed them as well. It must have been the will of the Father that they died because I still had not come to my senses at the time and was still in grieving for those that would perish from this evil darkness.

Even our family priest was no match from what he would call the evil one's 'grasping hands'. He prayed and prayed for anyone that came to us and he assured us that open fire pits and flames would repeal this darkness from touching our house, but as you will see, the darkness ended up devouring all that could not resist it. And upon its touch, one would surely die a long and horrible death that oftentimes drove its victims insane due to the unending pain from the touch of the darkness which ravaged the various organs of their bodies.

Our local healers couldn't understand how this darkness began and tried to do everything within their power to repulse it, but alas even they failed to withstand the darkness's hunger. At the time, I didn't understand or know how the darkness had spread among our ranks so quickly because it seemed to have two distinct symptoms. One group would break out in what appeared to be boils and then they would explode into pus filled nodules and leak out body fluids and the others would have teeth marks upon their necks, arms or inner thighs as though they had been attacked while working their fields, taverns or homes.

These two patterns would not be understood by any of us for years. What would cause such death? What would cause such markings upon a human body? How could we stop this darkness from consuming our whole land? And what kind of plague or demon could be consuming the blood of helpless innocents? And what confused us most was that many of those with the markings on them were sick with the darkness. Who would touch a defiled body that was so near death especially when 6 out of 10 that had contracted the darkness were destined to die by this attack of the evil one? I remember my prayers that I had often prayed with our family priest. 'Oh, dear Father, protect my people and kill whatever this creature is that is trying to feed upon them in these dark days of our trials. Oh, God, help us! Help us! I'm so afraid.' And then my priest would anoint me with oil and make me walk between four lit fires that seemed to be as hot as hell with the amount of heat they were putting out. And yet, while I had faith in Father Millinus, I was still praying, 'Father, please, I'm so afraid. Please spare my Father, Mother and my baby sisters from this evil darkness.' But

DAREN LESTER

I always wondered if God was listening to my prayers or what sin had we committed to bring this evil darkness upon us all. Was this the end of the world or just the end of our world? Only God knows the answer to that and He was my last hope against this creeping darkness that had consumed our village.

CHAPTER 2

T he darkness falls.
The very next morning after I had said my fervent prayers with our local priest, I arose to see that snow had covered the ground of our village. There was the basic hustle and bustle still going on during the day, but the night seemed to grow ever darker.

As I was dressing for the day in my ornate dress of blue and purple with gold and silver lining, I had two young maidens curling my hair and placing it up as it should be placed so I might conduct my daily business in our castle.

My first duty was to go and check in on the servants in the kitchen to make sure that the day's meals were going to be ready to receive our important guests and emissaries from the local markets, or maybe from different neighboring towns and once in awhile a foreign land. But still seeing as I was considered a youth, I had to attend to these duties that I might learn how to govern as a leader.

My Father always said, 'the best leaders are the ones that know how to shoe a horse as well as the ones that know how to ride the horse.' So basically that was his way of saying that you must learn every job so you can understand the problems one might face while doing the job that we might be able to give good and right council on how to fix any given problem in a day when our people come to us for advice or seek judgment in any matter.

I looked at that advice as silly at the time, but now that I am a few hundred years older, I can relate to what my Father was saying, but I digress.

On my morning rounds with my ladies in waiting, I was heading down the hallway next to the great hall and I heard a great commotion. It sounded like some of our people were at the point of panic and maybe violence. I heard shouting and yelling and even thought I heard cursing and threatening in the presence of my Father. I thought to myself that it was highly unusual. Are we going to war or are the Turks threatening my Father and our kingdom again?

Are we being blackmailed by some outside power? Who would dare speak to my Father in such a manner and why would my Father have dismissed my Mother from the throne room in such a rush? Who was this great power that caused such a fuss in my Father's seat of power?

While I was thinking these thoughts, suddenly my Mother seemed to run past me in a rush with her bodyguards who were all dressed in royal blue. She suddenly stopped by me and said, 'Sahnedra, don't go into the throne room right now. Your Father and several advisers are discussing a very important state matter and are trying to comfort some of our citizens that have been attacked by some outside source or power.'

I responded and said, 'Mother, I've got some reports that I must give to Father and then I will leave them be.' She interrupted me and said, 'I forbid you to speak to your Father at this time.' And she motioned my royal guards who were all dressed in light red and purple to keep me from entering the royal hall that proceeds to the throne room.

I couldn't believe it! Here I was on the edge of finding out what was going on and my very own Mother ordered my own personal guards to keep me from entering my own Father's throne room. What is going on that my Mom would forbid me from speaking to my Father about the daily reports he requires me to deliver to him? I've never been forbidden to speak to my Father. I am a princess! I have rights and I want to do what I've been told to do. I spoke up to my Mother and said, "You have no right to speak to me that way. You have taken and ordered my own protectors to keep me from speaking to my Father. How dare you! I'm not some common barmaid or whore that you can just order around. I have duties and I am your daughter, so move out of my way!"

Suddenly, right in front of my ladies in waiting and my guards, her guards and all her entourage, she grabbed me by the arm and twisted me around and smacked me right on the side of my face. She then grabbed me by my jaws and pushed me roughly against the wall and said, "I will not tell you again. I am the queen and you will do as I your Mother command you. This is for your own good. Guards, take our lovely princess and lock her in her royal bed chamber until she can act like a princess should. I expect to be respected by everyone so don't ever talk to me that way again, or I might forget that you're my daughter and see how you like staying at the local inn for a few nights without all the benefits of your royal rank.

I'm doing this for your own good, Sahnedra, and yes, there are some things you don't need to see or know right now. You are still a child; a lady in waiting. I would hate to have to place you in a convent for a while so you would learn what it is like to be a servant to all of our people, not just your own family. Now you and your ladies bow to me and give me the proper respect that your queen is due."

So after I was so publicly humiliated and fighting back tears and not being able to look at my ladies or even my guards in the face, they all had their heads down so as not to see the red handprint upon my face or the tear that had been made by my Mother forcing me into the wall upon my blue dress. I bowed my head and got down on one knee and pleaded for my Mother's forgiveness and thanked her for her mercy and for her kind advice that one day I might be a better queen when my day comes.

My heart was so heavy that afternoon that my guards didn't speak at all. I knew they were ashamed of what they had witnessed. Old Humboldt who had served as my chief guard since my birth was unusually quiet. He felt pity on me. I could sense it when I glanced into his eyes. I could tell he was feeling sorry for me. He seemed to say that he felt the issue had been overdone and my Mother had stepped out just a little too far with her threats and her actions. Though I know he could nor would never say so because he was as loyal to me and my family as my dear dog Buddy. Yes, even Buddy my dear beloved beagle seemed to sense that I had been mistreated and hurt. I threw myself upon my bed and began to cry as my ladies each were placed into their rooms with the doors locked behind them and then as I saw old Humboldt look at me, he winked and said ever so softly, 'My dear love, this too shall pass.' And then he gently smiled and briefly placed his kind hand upon mine and left me in my room and locked the door behind him. I heard him order a four guard watch upon my door and a two guard watch upon my ladies' door for 24 hours a day until the queen decided when we could leave our chambers.

But as I said, I began to weep because my Mother had hardly ever laid a finger upon me and now she treats me like a runaway whore that was willing to give up her essence for money. She even threatened to throw me away in a convent as some commoner so I could as she stated serve the lowest of the low. Am I not a princess? Why would my Father allow such a thing? Why would she say such things in public before her entourage and mine? Why? The convent is a place for nuns and girls that need to be shown their place in the kingdom and sadly most are forgotten there. Why would my Mother abandon me? Was she looking upon me as a threat to the throne? Why would she threaten such punishment in a public setting for me just wanting to do my duties and talk to my Daddy? Why?

I guess what really hurt me the most that evening as I thought about it and as my tears began to dry on the side of my face with all my makeup going everywhere was the fact that I might have been cast out of my room and away from all my family, friends and dear Humboldt and my ever faithful dog, Buddy.

That evening as the day began to fade into night, my lock sprung open and Humboldt gently opened the door. Buddy rushed to meet him and Humboldt bowed down and rubbed his head and kissed him. He said, "Good old, faithful Buddy. It's good to have a good friend in times of sorrow. My dear sweet child, your Mother has summoned you to her quarters and seeks an audience with you privately. She said she has much to discuss with you alone." Humboldt continued, "I pray dear princess that you use wisdom and be as the good book says, 'wise as a serpent and yet harmless as a dove.' Give our dear queen the respect she deserves and remember there is much going on that you and I don't know about in the kingdom. Your Mother, if I might add, is only doing what she thinks is the best for you and all of us. I ask your forgiveness if I've spoken out of place."

I looked up from my bed and saw my ladies coming to me and they began to get a wash pan and clean the running makeup off my cheeks and started to find me a dress that would work for me. And as they were beginning to remove my makeup and began to remove my royal garments that were torn, Humboldt began to turn to leave the room. I spoke to him and said, "Dear Humboldt, may you and your wise advice live forever? Thank you for being a kind and gentle keeper of my path and God keep you in all your duties tonight." As he turned, he said, "Yes, my princess. One day when you are queen, please remember my family and all that I have done for you and your family and give my children a leave from the Royal Army. May my children never see war nor have to rise up a blade against either their own countrymen or those of other people. Long live my dear King and all that pertains to him." And I replied, "So be it. I will not forget your kindness to me this day."

And then the door shut behind him save for the royal guard that waited upon the outside of my door. It was all quiet now in the hallways. My ladies had taken my blue/purple dress off of me and had redone my makeup as well as placed upon me a lightly brown tinted dress with a tint of dark in it. My ladies advised me to go in before my Mother in a more common fashion that I might show her what I may look like as a more commoner if she placed me away for a season. They advised me to let her see what I would be like if I was no longer in the garb of a princess and maybe the shame of me going in before her in this manner would make her repent of such a possible judgment against me.

As I went to the door and knocked, my guards gently opened the door to my room from the other side. Trist, my second guard said, "Meek and gentle. This is good. May God shine upon you tonight and bring peace back between you and your Mother." Trist was a young man in his mid-twenties and yet it seemed like I knew him my whole life and now that I think about it, I did until the day he passed on to be with God.

Trist had taken command of my personal guard for the night and he called the guard to order and we began to walk in an orderly fashion to the queen's room. There, her guards met my guards and Justarly saluted me and Trist and we and my ladies passed on to my Mother's room. There my Mother was sitting and talking to her advisors about various issues. When I entered the room, they all stood up and bowed save for my Mother of course. She quietly asked for the room to be cleared of all present save for me and her. Trist and Justarly were the very last to leave and as they left, they bowed to us and went out backwards closing the doors behind them and the last thing I heard was the orders for the guards to be posted at the doors and that when the princess or queen needed anything for them to run with haste to fetch either Trist or Justarly or both at once.

Then, when the doors were latched, my Mother smiled at me and she winked and said, "I see you have put on some more common clothing. It doesn't become you my dear. You are my eldest daughter and you are important to me. I and your Father have and are grooming you to be a queen as it were someday and to be an asset to a duke, king or some such regent. But to do so, you must act like a princess and watch what you do and what you say. I know that you know this already and in most cases you have, but you will not act against any of my words. If you have a thought, then bring it to me in private. We must not show weakness at this time. This is a time of trouble for us and our small kingdom. Your Father has decided to call up the army to full strength and setup seeking a reserve. We don't know if we are under attack, if someone is trying to infiltrate us with disease or assassins or if this is some prelude to an all-out invasion."

My Mother continued, "All we know for sure is that we have sent out spies and all have came back with the same reports. This thing, whatever or whoever is behind it is seeming to happen all around us and we are in the middle of it. We have sent men up and down rivers into the neighboring towns, cities, countries and even to the land of the Turks and it seems that a combination of sickness, disease and death is taking place. And yet, it's more than just a plague or illness that is killing dozens and dozens of people. It's like someone or a group of bandits or something is taking advantage of this situation to rob and plunder the neighboring lands. And by rob, I don't mean stuff such as gold, silver, cattle and chickens but people. All strands of people from priests, nuns, soldiers, commoners and worst of all, royals.

We've not just seen signs of it starting on our trade routes east, but also in the north, south and west all around us. We know the plague and are taking all the steps our healers can think of to deal with it, but something is also attacking. Sick and helpless people along the trails, paths and highways of all the states that border us.

Your Father thought it was some evil drummed up by the Turks, but our spies saw a caravan of Turks on the highway that had been decimated by someone or something. An Imam and his party had their throats ripped out a few paces after that and a group of peasants had also been attacked. Your Father and his advisors are so worried about the attacks that he has made the difficult choice of beginning to round up all of the men and boys capable of fighting from the ages of twelve to sixty for military service. They fear the Turks will blame these random attacks upon us and our small kingdom as an excuse to attack us."

Then I asked, "Mother, may I speak?" My Mother nodded and I said, "Mother, who would dare attack us? The neighboring countries? And even if they dared such, then who would dare trouble the Turks? They are a power of powers at this time and no one seeks war with them unless it is out of madness." She nodded and replied, "We just don't know, but you must purport yourself as a princess and do not show weakness of any kind at this time because our people must have faith in their king and their queen and all its royal line. If they don't have faith in us to deal with this external or internal problem, then we may be overthrown, exiled or worse, killed and beheaded.

Your Father is planning to raise a 30,000 strong frontline army with about 10-15,000 strong home guard. Hopefully, this will be enough to scare off whatever or whoever it is that is attacking our trade routes. We intend to begin sending forceful patrols up and down the lines of our land and we intend to contact via emissaries all the surrounding countries and tell them what we are doing and that we intend no threats or harm to anyone but we are seeking peaceful security. This is our hope and prayer and we also pray that the Turks do not use this as an excuse to invade us. We hope they won't view this as a moment of weakness and strike north again. But whatever happens, it is all in the hands of our God. Father Millinus and several local priests are leading prayers in the chapel and anointing your Father and his advisors as leader of Heaven's army. All we can do is pray that Heaven will fight with us and help us overcome this descending darkness that seems to be falling upon our land and the neighboring region."

At the conclusion of my speaking with her, she motioned me near and I fell on my knees with tears flowing down my cheeks and said, "Mother, I'm sorry. I didn't know. I wanted to find out what all the shouting was about and I was just, well, just curious. Please forgive me."

She then took me by the hand and held me to her bosom and began to rub my dark hair ever so gently but firmly and said to me, "Oh, my dear sweet Sahnedra, you are the light of this kingdom and you and your sisters are the hope of the future. All the children of this kingdom are more valuable than all the silver and gold that might ever be mined out of the earth. Know your Father and I love you all and are willing to go to hell and back to protect all of our kingdom's children from whatever the threat that comes our way. Whether in this world or the next, we will win because we have to."

With that, she held me back by my shoulders and kissed me on the cheek and said, "Get out of these drab clothes and tomorrow, I want to see you in a royal dress, one befitting a princess." And with a final hug and a quick smack on the cheek, my Mother summoned Justarly and Trist and I was escorted back to my room.

But all that night, I had questions about what was this plague. Who caused it? Who would dare attack a kingdom that was willing to fight for its right to exist? Did they even know these things? Were there spies in our midst? Would they back down? Would they even care that we are beginning to prepare for war? These things kept the sleep from coming to me that night. The night before my world began to shake.

CHAPTER 3

My world was shaken.

I never will forget that night that I was escorted to my bed chambers and had just lain down. Sleep seemed to elude my eyes no matter what I did. I just couldn't get my mind to stop thinking on what was going on around our small little kingdom. I got up and ran to the kitchen and fetched me a small cup of warm tea and hoped that this would put my mind at ease at least enough so I could fall asleep. At this point, I wouldn't have cared if I slept an entire day. It just seemed that I never was able to truly rest anymore and then I would start thinking about my dear Father, Mother and sisters and how they must have felt. I prayed that Father would be able to rest and that his mind wasn't always upon all the stress that he faced in his day to day dealings with the sickness that was attacking all the surrounding lands and the constant threat of war with the nearby Turks. I prayed for Mother that she would be able to maintain her royal mannerisms so she could be as useful to Father in diplomacy as she was as a wife.

I prayed for my sisters that their minds wouldn't be overwhelmed with the issues of the day and instead they could concentrate upon being young ladies and doing all the fun things that young ladies do.

But it seemed as though these prayers of mine were not to be. That something else also had dreams and desires for my family, my people and yes, myself. But as I finally felt my eyes start to close that night, I could help but wonder what was truly going on. Has the end of the world begun? Is this God's judgment upon all of us for some sin that we as a people have committed? Was Father Millinus wrong? Was there even a God that cared about what was happening here on earth?

All these questions raced through my mind at a rapid pace and yet I couldn't seem to find answers that would put my mind at rest. The next morning I was awakened by Mercia our chamber maid as she gently knocked on the door and asked if she was allowed to enter the room.

I answered and said, "Come on in, I'm awake." and then Mercia opened the door and said that breakfast would be ready in thirty minutes and if I didn't mind she would like to get started changing my bed linens and dust the room. I said, "Do whatever it is that you must. I've got to hurry and get dressed and go get breakfast so I can get my daily chores started and finished hopefully early so I can spy out what the young men look like down in the center of town who are being brought up for Father's army."

Mercia smiled and said, "Hopefully all of the young men will be able to go home soon to be with their families and all of them return home safe and unharmed." I nodded in agreement with her and said, "Yes, I would hate to hear of anyone being killed or hurt fighting over a mere misunderstanding or something of that nature."

Mercia then said, "Hurry, child, you're needed in the dining area and you don't want to be late again. You know how your Mother hates it when you children dilly-dally around and make your Father wait to eat his breakfast. Each minute you make him late is another minute he will be out away doing business in the evening."

So I leapt out of bed, grabbed my dress and put it on as I raced to the dining area. As I walked through the hallway, I saw guards in great numbers. All of them were heavily armed and standing at attention as though they were prepared for an attack. I asked Trist what is going on and he said, "Hurry, Sahnedra, and go to breakfast. Your Father will tell you what is going on."

So I glided past the guards and slipped into the dining area and as I was preparing to sit down, I could see my Mother glaring at me with her eyes and I couldn't help but think, Oh, boy, here we go again! This is going to go one of three ways:

1. She will say nothing and forget I'm a few seconds late. 2. She will ask me why I'm late and then give me a lecture about me not being punctual and about needing to set a better example for my younger sisters or 3. She will ask me to leave the room and come back later on when I'm hungry enough to eat at lunch time. I hated the 3rd option because then I would have to work all morning and not be able to think right because my stomach would be growling all day. And I sure didn't want to go watch the young men drilling in the center of town with an empty stomach. I mean, what if one of the ladies in waiting heard it, then I would never hear the end of it. My young friends were always teasing me the way it was. The three of them never gave me a bit of space. It was princess this, princess that. Oh, I wish some days to leave all this drab behind and just be able to be just a young lady without all of the pretense and garb that went along with being a royal. But as I was waiting to see what my Mother would do to me, I noticed she just suddenly smiled at me but I couldn't help but notice that Catherine, Elia and Miranda were all sitting and giggling at me as I was preparing to give my Mother an answer. I think that they must have seen me swallow hard or something because I could feel a sigh of relief just by having my Mother look at me and wink while I sat quietly down.

Father was whispering to Humboldt about something and he had a look of concern that I don't think I've ever seen upon his face since I've known him. Buddy was just sitting beside my feet on the floor begging for me to throw him a biscuit or for that matter, anything anyone did not want. Buddy wasn't a picky dog; he was just a good dog. If you gave him a bone he would eat it. If you threw him a bowl of soup, he would slurp it all down. My dear beagle wasn't very bright, but he was my dog and that is all that mattered to me because I knew in my heart that Buddy would give his life for me if I ever needed him and I would do the same for him. Buddy was the kind of friend that one could only dream about. I could tell him anything and he would never talk to anyone about it. What a friend indeed.

Now as I continued to scan the table trying to catch a whisper of what was going on, I noticed that Myra and Vilian were poking each other and pulling at each other's hair until Mother arose and said, "If you don't get a hold of yourselves, I will have you leave this table and make you go work in the garden today." Well, being told this shut them and their nonsense down quick. Vilian the youngest said, "Mother, that's not fair! That is why we have servants." Mother then replied, "If you want to not be one, then act like you are supposed to act. What kind of prince is going to want to marry a princess that can't keep her hands off another princess? I mean, tell me who would marry a princess that can't keep her hair nice and untangled? I'll tell you, no one! Prepare yourselves as you've been instructed and watch my words you will both marry a handsome young prince someday. I still have high hopes for you. Now, Sahnedra, you on the other hand, I wonder some days. Will you ever stop goofing off and take your station seriously?" My response was of course, "Mother, I will. I just like to have fun sometimes too." She responded to me and said, "I've seen you and your three companions going out to watch the young men drill after you've got your chores done. Now do you think that is a wise thing to do?" I answered, "Mother, I just wanted to watch Trist put them through their paces. I meant no harm." Mother responded, "Of course you didn't, but you and your friends might distract the young men. Let's face it, you are all the most beautiful women in the kingdom. So let's try and keep ourselves from distracting Father's young men so they can focus and keep our kingdom safe, okay?" Myself and Catherine, Elia and Miranda all said "Yes, ma."

Father then noticed no one was eating because he had as yet prepared his plate due to the fact he kept having advisors come and go giving Humboldt and himself constant updates about whatever was taking place in the kingdom. So Father abruptly said, "Hold on now, Father Millinus, please ask grace for the food and pray for the safety of our kingdom."

So, Father Millinus rose up and said, "Please bow your heads and begin to give thanks for the food God has provided for us" and also he asked God's direction and guiding hand upon Father and Humboldt and all of the men of the kingdom as they see to the protection of our kingdom.

Then as Father Millinus sat down, Father rose and said, "It is a sad day. One of our small villages has been completely destroyed. Who, what or how we don't know, but as of now, I'm having Humboldt gather together two hundred of our choice men that he and myself might go to the village and see for ourselves what has happened. As of this day, I consider our kingdom in a state of war."

Mother rose up and said, "How can you, Dargon? Who are we at war with? If you start sending troops out, then you might upset our neighbors and they might think we are going to attack them. Do you really think this is wise to just go and start marching around the kingdom at this time in battle formations?"

Father stood still for a moment and said, "Vinician, you are a good wife, but we have no choice and I expect your full public support in this matter. What I do I do with the consent of Father Millinus and the church as well as Humboldt and his chief soldiers as well. I personally believe it is better to be safe than sorry and that a strong early show of force will put the invisible enemy to flight perhaps saving lives in the long run. I will lead the small force myself and this should show them that the kingdom is fully behind the decision that I've made and in so doing perhaps we can avoid further bloodshed and maybe we can find out who is behind these senseless attacks and bring them to trial or kill them if need be and end this issue once and for all."

So Mother sat down and Humboldt arose and said, "All hail the King!" and everyone in the room did accordingly and then he and Father sat down and we all began to eat. Needless to say, I had a hard time eating as did everyone else because we all knew that this could lead to a broader war and we all knew that it may be a war that we as a small kingdom couldn't win no matter how strong our army was or how bravely our men fought. We might provoke powers that were vastly stronger than us. Oh, God, I thought in my mind. Please help us and protect us from the powers that are plaguing us at this time.

After breakfast, Father and Father Millinus as well as Humboldt all arose and went out to the front gate and mounted horses with two hundred of our army's choices and they began to ride off to the small village of Vinalus. I hoped I would see my Father and the men return home soon safe and sound and that the report of the attack would be proven to be wrong.

Well, as I turned my back and started to go about doing my daily chores, I noticed that snow had started to fall yet again and that the ground was all muddy. The sky was dark and it seemed as though night was already setting in upon us. Yes, I know we had just had breakfast, but it just seemed as of late that darkness never left the sky. Oh, well, soon in a few months spring will come and all will be well yet again.

Dargon's Journal Entry:

We finally arrived at Vinalus. It took about six hours of hard riding and the bad weather didn't help things out either. As we entered the village, this is what I saw. There was no life whatsoever. The village was totally empty. Not a soul to be found or so we thought at first. I ordered my men to spread out in companies of three of roughly sixty-six men each. I would lead one company then Father Millinus would be the lead the second and of course Humboldt would lead the third company. We decided after talking about it to enter the village from three different directions so as we might surprise any lingering enemy forces that might have remained behind to loot the village.

So as I rode in with my men at the front of the village, I ordered my men to dismount and to proceed on foot. I ordered ten men to guard and care for our horses and protect them with their lives in case we had to withdraw in a hurry. So I and fifty-six men began to proceed to the village on foot. As we entered the village, we saw just empty homes and stores with pots and pans everywhere.

A few weapons were lying around and house fires seemed to still be burning in a few of the homes but no person was on the side of the village we took. No animals remained, but yet all the food stores, furniture, homes, gold and silver that was in the homes remained. I thought to myself, what kind of invasion is this? Are they just after slaves and animals? What kind of invading army would take the people but not possess the land or not take or loot the food or gold or silver? It's winter for God's sake and an army travels on its stomach. Even pack animals have to eat and yet they didn't even take any hay that is laid up in the barns. What is going on here?

Well, as I was taking in all that I saw, I noticed that Father Millinus rode in charging with his men on horseback. He had arrived from the hills around the village to the north and we began to talk and he told me that he saw no sign of open warfare. No sign of a siege or any kind of looting. And then Humboldt arrived having approached from the east side of the village and his furrowed brow gave me a deep concern.

He said, "My lord, this makes no sense. There are no signs of war at all. It's like these people were picked off. I don't see a whole lot of weapons laying around and I have seen empty wagons and some cattle on the east side of the village as we approached, but each and every home we inspected was empty. How can a village of one hundred plus people just disappear? I've been about the game of war for a long time and any army that invades in winter always takes captives but they leave the dead on the ground. The Turks showcase their victories and no army would leave empty wagons. The wagons would be filled with the spoils of war and yet no spoils have been taken except maybe the people. Who could capture a whole village so quick? Some of our people would have put up a fight. I had ten men here just to patrol the border area and not one of them made it back to me to give me a report of any kind of attack. This makes no sense at all."

So then I told Humboldt to have the men search every house and make an account of all of the items in the homes. I sent back ten men to the castle and ordered them to bring back twenty-five more with them.

We were going to gather up all of the supplies that this village had and store them in Satu Mare and in this way, no enemy would gather up what our people had worked so hard for over the spring and summer. I ordered them to load up the wagons and don't leave one piece of cut wood behind. As my men were cleaning out the food stores and all of the equipment and weapons we could find, I couldn't help but notice that there were some signs in various places of a struggle and drippings of blood here and there. When all of the sudden, Father Millinus said, "Sir, we have loaded up all we can on the wagons and horses and now all we have to do is wait on the other men you summoned to arrive. But I think it would be advisable to take refuge in the homes tonight and wait on the men to arrive early tomorrow."

I agreed after consulting with Humboldt and we began to deploy the men in homes and place grounds around and I also had the men set fires throughout the village in a hopeful attempt to deceive any possible foe about the strength we currently had with us and thus hopefully would make them think we had ten times as many men as we currently did.

As I sat at a table eating with some of my men, I began to dictate letters to various generals over our army about what we had seen and asking them to make reports to myself every week from this day forward as to any weird or important issue.

Suddenly, I heard a man shout, "Alert to arms!" So I and my men arose and ran out the door grabbing our weapons and placing our armor on as we ran. We ran to where the noise was and we found a young man with his sword drawn and ready to attack. I grabbed him and said, "What did you see? How many? Where from? Which direction?"

He said, "Sir, look, we saw a young lady crawling up the hill towards us. I ordered Humboldt to take a few men and get her. Maybe we can finally figure out what is going on around here."

Humboldt and his men ran by the light of their torches to where they saw the young lady and he grabbed her up in his arms and began to run back to us. When all of the sudden, arrows began to rain out from the sky behind them. I yelled to Humboldt and told my men to get into formation to repel attackers. As I yelled, Humboldt fell down and was hit in his back by an arrow. Eight of the men who were with him made it back to our lines and joined into rank formation. Humboldt was still alive and struggling to get back up on his feet. But then, without warning, the young girl appeared to get up and grab him by the neck and it seemed as though she bit him there. Humboldt screamed out in agony and I ordered my men to advance, but we had to stop because arrows began to rain down all around us to no effect but still the danger was too great to advance against an unseen enemy in the dark.

As I watched, Humboldt was released by the young lady and he slumped to the ground. I ordered her to stop and all the while arrows were whizzing past me and my men and seemed to strike this young woman without having much effect upon her. I grabbed a javelin and took aim and hurled it at her. It hit her in the leg and she fell down for a moment and then began to run towards us. Father Millinus said to aim at her heart because she is a night creature so I took another javelin and aimed and hurled it at her and this time my aim was good and she fell down dead.

I yelled out to those that were shooting arrows at us to stop and declare themselves. Then the arrows stopped and a small band of Turks came out of the woods. They immediately ran up and cut off the head of Humboldt and the young lady. I and my men advanced and said, "Who are you and why are you on my land?"

The young Turkish lieutenant answered, "My name is Humood, son of Humilluom. I and my men were on patrol near our borders over the last few weeks when a band of people seemed to leap out of the trees and pull us off our horses and began attacking us like wild animals. We who survived followed them as far as here. I thought that perhaps your kingdom had attacked us but I can see that I was wrong and that your kingdom as well as our own has been the victims of some great evil."

I asked, "Humood, have you eaten?" and he said that he and six soldiers had not eaten in days because every time they tried to settle down they would always be attacked. He also told me that he was part of a patrol that used to contain around thirty-five men but that they were all that was left and he had hoped to see what had been attacking them before he returned back to his governors territory with a full report.

I asked Humood to shelter with us that night and that we would let him abide in a empty home and we could go our separate ways in the morning and he agreed and he said that he would give a report that the attacks that had plagued his land were not coming from us but that we had been attacked as well and we needed to trade information that we both might put an end to these needless murders.

Well, the night seemed to be peaceful enough but as morning shot up over the hills, it couldn't have been soon enough for me. As I arose, I heard horse hooves coming down the road and the clinking and clanking of heavy armor coming. And as I looked up, I noticed the troops I had requested were about to arrive, but some of the men appeared weak and sickly looking.

I asked Trist what had happened and he said that they had killed a wild acting man last night as they traveled to the village. He said the man tore out the throats of three of his men and wounded another before they finally put the man down for good. Trist explained that they shot the man with arrows and stabbed him repeatedly with swords and spears and the man wouldn't stay down until one of the men finally stabbed the man with a spear through his heart.

Trist told me that he had never seen anything like it that each time an arrow hit the man he would just pull it out and it seemed as though he healed very quickly. Trist also showed me the young man that had been bitten upon the arm. It was just a small mark and Father Millinus poured holy water upon it and placed a hot iron over it to try to prevent infection.

The young man's name was Ralisu and we asked him if he felt okay and he replied that he did but that he was seeing the sun in sort of a haze over his eyes and that he felt dizzy and weak today. So, I told him to take some rest while we loaded up the rest of the wagons. Humood and his men bid us farewell and said they would be sure to have their governor contact us so we could compare stories about what we seemed to be facing.

Trist told me he believed that the Black Death was responsible for the issues we all were facing and that as soon as we treat and banish this evil disease, all would be back to normal but Father Millinus said he had read about this before in the books of the early Roman Empire and that he believed it was some risen creatures of the dark coming to reap the souls of men for their own need. I didn't know what to think except that it was hard to put them down unless you hit them in the heart or cut off their heads.

I am completely confused. This seems like such a dream and I on this day of our Lord have ordered the complete destruction of the village of Vinalus. Father Millinus recommended that we burn the village to the ground to help fight the plague and that we raise up a cross over the town to sanctify it against any more evil that might seek to inhabit the town after we leave. So I ordered the town to be burnt and we raised a cross over it and during this time, I ordered Trist to escort the loot out of the town and then I returned to Satu Mare and he went to order each village, town and city to close all of their gates and post guards upon every wall to protect them against wild beast men.

I have also issued on this day of our Lord that we are currently in a state of war with unknown forces of darkness and how one can kill the dark ones and I request if any find other ways to kill any dark creatures that it be sent in haste to your lord and King Dargon as this is my royal decree.

That night as I and Father Millinus were riding home in the dark towards Satu Mare, Ralisu fell off of his horse. I ordered a soldier to get off of his horse and to see if the young man was all right and as the young man approached him, he bent down and felt his skin and said he is cold to the touch. So Father Millinus said the last rights over the boy and we laid him upon the ground and placed rocks over him and then proceeded upon our way home to the city.

After several more hours, I said to Father Millinus, "How are you doing?" and he said, "I could use a rest" so I ordered our company of twenty-five men to stop and dismount and to make camp and that we would continue the rest of the journey to Satu Mare tomorrow morning early.

Well, the night was uneventful and we got up well rested but still on edge after all that had happened within the last few nights and I couldn't stop wondering why I had such vivid yet wild dreams last night. Father Millinus and several of the men seemed paler than usual and one of our company was missing. We searched the surrounding fields and woods for hours and couldn't find any signs of our missing man. So we figured we should head back and give a report to all of our advisors in the castle and come up with a plan as to how to clear out any signs of plague of evil in our kingdom.

As I rode into the city, I couldn't help but notice that Sahnedra was anxiously watching for me from her bed chambers window and that she started waving at me as we approached. Then her sisters and her ladies joined her and oh, yes, there she is, my dear wife. My dear Vinician. I've never been so glad to be home and thank God we made it in one piece and now we can take and relax for a day or two as we decide how to deal with the issues facing the kingdom.

Suddenly, I saw Father and shouted to him, "Daddy, welcome home! I've missed you and I can't wait to see you and Father Millinus!" Wait, I wonder where Humboldt is, I thought to myself. I don't see Humboldt. Where could he be? What's going on? Did he leave him to guard the village? That must be it! He must have left him in charge of securing the border. Maybe I can go see him and make sure he is okay. Maybe Buddy and I can take him some cakes to him and his men and thank them for keeping us all safe. That's what I will do. Oh, please hurry Father! I want to talk to you! Get out of the way, Catherine! Stop trying to look at Trist and get his attention!

Trist was a handsome man but ten years my elder so he would never be interested in a younger woman probably and besides, Mother would probably forbid me to see him anyway. She had higher goals for me and my life. She expected me to be perfect and to be able to break down walls and be able to obtain positions of heights that she would never attempt to reach herself. Why couldn't she just allow me to set my own goals and find my own way through life? Who would ever have been able to imagine that a mere few more months and our world would no longer be as it had been and that what was would never be again?

Who could imagine that the winds were changing and that the cold of death was only as cold as the one that brought it into our lives. Sometimes mercy is another means for death to enter one's life. I will never forget that mercy had no pity upon me the night my life ended abruptly. Are you ready to see what mercy did to me?

CHAPTER 4

Mercy?

As I began to run down the corridor to try and get to the stairs, I couldn't help but keep grabbing at Catherine's hand to make sure she was still close to me. We both wanted to run as quickly as possible so that we could see what was the word concerning our kingdom.

Was our kingdom at war? Were we at peace? Did we meet with the Turks and the other bordering powers? Did we find out who or what was spreading this disease to our people? All these and a thousand other questions were swirling through my head like the wind blows the leaves in the fall. I just could seem to grab on one single thought and focus. It seemed like Daddy, Humboldt, Trist and the men that were with them had been gone for a thousand years and I wanted to be among the first to say welcome home.

As Catherine and I ran down the stairs, we finally got to the front door where Mother was already standing anxiously awaiting word from Father and Humboldt about how things went and hopeful word as to the avoidance of possible war with outside threats.

Meanwhile, Father and his men were still slowly riding in what seemed to Mother and I as in a procession formation. Mother asked one of the men why they would be riding home in such a slow manner and why they would choose such a formation if all was well.

The officer of the court said, "My queen, if they are using the formation of the fallen, then we have had some casualties and some of our men have fallen in battle or have been attacked by this insidious disease."

Mother grimaced and placed her hand quickly but silently over her mouth and then silently glanced around and removed it most likely trying to hide her fearful concern for what might have happened on the recent journey. I could tell that Mother was probably dealing with the stress and worry about what might have happened or what may still befall us if the worst case were to happen. But Mother was a strong woman and she seemed to quickly be able to regain her composure and put herself aright and return to the silent but strong figure of a woman that a queenly monarch should be or at least that is what we were always told.

As Father and his troops continued up to the cobblestone road that leads to the front gate of the castle, he slowed even more and we could see what appeared to be three empty horses but no bodies. That was odd. Usually if our kingdom lost men in a fight, they tried with all their might to retain or retake a fallen body and bring it back home to the family. Why didn't Father bring back the bodies? Was it disease concerns? Was it because they couldn't find them? What? While my mind began to race with yet another thousand questions, suddenly, Father Millinus dismounted his horse and began to run to us. He quickly stopped by the brothers of his Sacred Order-(the Order of High Palin) which went about trying to aid and heal the sick as much as the Most High would allow them.

Then after a brief but lingering stop to confer with his Order, he began to look at Mother and myself and all those that were at the front entrance of the castle. He began to solemnly walk to us and I could tell that he was debating how to tell us what had happened and how to put it in just the right words. I have seen this walk before and when Father Millinus is slow to greet people then it means a lot. It means that the world must have been shaken and he is at a loss as to how to deal with the situation that is befallen the family or in this case it must be the whole kingdom.

"Oh, come on Father Millinus, what is going on?" I shouted. Mother quickly glanced at me with a stare that said without saying to keep my composure and allow the good father to come to us and brief us at the Lord's time. Then just as quickly as I got the stare to be quiet, my Mother grabbed my hand and Catherine's as if to say, "I know, girls. I want to know what happened as well."

Finally after a few more moments, Father Millinus came up to all who were at the entrance gate of the main court of the castle. He stood still and silent staring out as for what seemed to be an eternity. Then he began to softly speak and say, "Well, the good news is that we are not at war with the Turks or any other kingdom and this blight has seemingly affected them as well. If you can call that good news which being a priest I think I may want to pray about my idea of good news. Being glad that this awful blight is affecting others...dear Lord help me." Mother moved up and grabbed Father Millinus's hand and said, "Yes, yes, Father, the Lord knows what you meant. You're not glad to see anyone affected with evil in any way. But what happened out there and why did it take you a few weeks to get back on what should have been a three to four day journey at most?"

Father Millinus seemed to snap out of his rambling and said, "Dear ones, here is what has gone on. We lost three and maybe four men on this scouting journey and sadly the one we lost first was Humboldt. He fell when an evil, possessed woman attacked him and tore his neck and then we lost two to three others in the night and we searched whole areas in force for them for days. The reason I say possibly four men is a young man named Ralisu was bitten by one of the inferno beast people that are spreading this sickness and he is in fever.

That is why I stopped by my Order so that I could have them ready to receive him and to give him the best care possible that my

Order and the kingdom can give. I wanted them to lock him away and to keep three priests as guards around him at all times just in case something goes wrong. At least we can try and help him and hopefully protect our people at the same time by trying to limit contact with the infected."

Then I and Mother and all those that were with us began to cry because Humboldt was a lifelong, dear friend that had been in our court for what seemed like forever. He was just always around seeing to our protection and our comfort. He made sure the kingdom was always kept safe and whatever was reported was given directly to the king's ear after he received word from the rider or bearer of the news.

"Humboldt!" I cried out, "How could you have fallen? How could you be gone?" I loved him like an older and wiser brother, father and most of all a dear friend that I could confide in when no one else seemed to care or would have listened. "Humboldt, our world is now darker because your light is no more."

I cried and cried so much that Father Millinus who rarely hugs anyone came over to me and said, "Child, I know it is a grievous loss, but he is now better off than we are because he is now one of God's guardian angels. What he could not do for us in life, God may allow him to do for us in eternity. He is now with the great gatekeeper Saint Peter and knowing my good friend Humboldt, he will see to it that no devil ever enters the Kingdom of God. Now stay strong. I have to go and speak to his family concerning this issue and I will need your prayers because this is more than my heart can bear. They have lost a husband, father and provider, but I have lost a friend and confidant that will not soon be replaced. May God help me because it is hard to bear awful news at any time especially when it is that of a dear friend that you have been raised with and his family all your life."

As Father Millinus let go of me, he began to walk away patting my sisters and those around us each one on our shoulders as if to say it will all be well soon enough. He gave last minute instructions to some of the men and he glanced at Trist and said, "You are now number one and Drang is your second. I want the both of you to meet me in six hours for a meeting to discuss what has taken place and what we should do. Be sure to grab Father Millinus and make sure to have him check on Ralisu so that he can tell us about his condition."

Trist nodded and turned to go and find Drang who was a younger man, but had been following Humboldt around since he joined the royal guard. And he quickly caught Father's attention because he always seemed to be cool headed and paid close attention to detail and could figure out those hard things that most people would try and avoid. No, Drang seemed to look forward to the challenges and he seemed to almost look to find them. But he was an odd choice for second because there were so many more in line that Father could have chosen that were in our service many more years than this relative newcomer.

Meanwhile, as Trist began to gather up the men and call them to formation, Father came to us and as he was being disarmored, he said, "I guess you have heard of our losses and of our sick one that was attacked but not killed by an evil person beast?"

Mother said, "Dargon, what happened?" So Father said, "Mother, this is the story." And as he began to talk to us, he grabbed Mother's hand and began to lead her away from the group where I was. I really hate that when that happens! Don't I deserve to know what happened? Am I not a princess being groomed like a sheep for the role of leadership? What a lack of respect! So as Father and Mother began to walk away, I quietly began to follow them all the while noticing the silent stars of my sisters, friends and guards who attempted to grab me, but I looked at them and said, "Don't touch me. I'm in need of important information and I am going to get it or else." So the guard who had tried to softly restrain me let me loose and I quickly caught up with Father and Mother. Then Father noticed that he and Mother were not alone and he said, "Sahnedra, why do you follow me seeing I desire to talk to your Mother alone concerning matters of the kingdom?" I responded, "Because I'm third in line and if something happens to you or Mother, I may need this information to lead the people as you or Mother would."

He looked at me for a while and then he smiled while Mother gazed at him to see what he would say. He replied, "Very wise. I do believe my little one is growing up and beginning to understand her role in the kingdom. But not yet. I will have Father Millinus or Trist inform you of what is important for you to know when it is time. Some things are just too important to have out there for the birds to snatch up and fly away with." After saying that, he winked at me and waved me off.

I slowly turned around and thought, Wow, he complimented me but then he blew me off saying he couldn't trust me with information. Wow, what just happened here?? So I started back down the hall so as not to see anyone that had looked at me when I decided to take my perilous trip after my parents. I walked up the stairs and down the hall to my room where I went in and sat at my dressing mirror for a few minutes.

Trist having called the men to formation began to call roll and the men of the castle answered one by one to their name and place of birth. He then proceeded to execute the orders of the king after having told the men in confidence about the losses of their friends and countrymen. Then, when he received a question as to who was now the first and who would be the second, he promptly answered and said, "I've taken the first position of course as should be expected, but our king has chosen to skip formalities and promote Drang to second." This immediately caused a stir among the men. One spoke up and said, "What about Clive? He was the third and if not him, then shouldn't it have been at least Stimer because he was our fourth?" Trist spoke up and said, "Yes, settle down. The promotion of Drang is not because he deserves it by right of rank, but because he is wanted by our king because of his talents for figuring out hard things. The king said that his skills may be needed in a more direct light with what we are facing and this promotion will limit the need to pass information to him through others and thus protect our kingdom's secrets as well as limit who knows what and when. Again, in an effort to limit information accidently passing out by the way of gossip or meal talk."

"I want you men to know that this promotion was not my choice and I spoke to the king about why I believe Clive or Stimer should have gotten the promotion by right of time served and knowledge of tactics and battle formations. They will still retain their ranks and will each receive an increase in pay for their faithful service and their lack of promotion in no way reflects their inability to do the job of second. It's just that in the king's mind at this time our kingdom needs an extraordinary mind for an extraordinary time. We can't fight whatever it is we are facing using usual armed protocols. We have to move outside the realm of direct armed forces as much as possible and that may include magic, prayer, medicine and armed force, but it will be a combination of all along with a healthy dose of diplomacy with the other kingdoms to confine this threat that is a threat to us all and then to deal and hopefully fully destroy this threat."

"Sir, spoke Clive, sir, I don't mean to interrupt you, but what threat? Isn't this just another form of the plague?" "No, Clive, that it is not. We do know that it is spread by person to beast to people which may mean it is some sort of disease, but since we are dealing with a person or persons, it means we must look at it as some sort of attack and war. Really, we don't know what is going on. The person beast that we saw was killed and we hoped that would be the end of it, but we lost a couple of other men in the first night that we were sleeping at our camp. I hope sadly that what took the men were some wolves or bears or something along those lines and not a person beast. Wolves, bears and cats I can deal with and hunt down if they are a menace, but a person beast is altogether different." Stimer spoke up and said, "Trist sir, if that is the case, then why don't we go out and hunt these wild person beasts?" Trist stated, "The answer is simple. It would appear that a person beast may be able to act normal when they want and then they can and do attack you at their time of choosing. All this information came to us by the way of Humood who is an lieutenant in the Turk army. He told us that he had a large group of men patrolling the borders of his lands originally and they picked up a woman that appeared to them to be in need of help. He said that she appeared to be unable to walk and that she stated she could not stand up but had to crawl because she had been attacked by a man and a woman that had been walking with her for miles. And then suddenly they attacked her and bit her. They had told her she was lucky they didn't just drain her life out of her, but that they wanted to play with her and might come back at any time to finish the job or they might just leave her alone and let her die in the night.

The lieutenant and his men picked her up and placed her upon a horse and were trying to escort her back to her village while they were setting up camp and getting ready to set guards for the night as well as to eat and rest. The woman began to want to go lie down, so they set up a tent for her and she went off to sleep or so the Turks thought. It would appear that the woman went off to sleep and then sometime during the night arose up out of the tent and killed that one night alone half a dozen men. Mostly while they were half asleep or while they were asleep. He is unsure how one woman could have done that to trained, battle hardened soldiers of the Turk army but never the less, it happened."

Trist continued, "We don't know if the woman did it or if she was aided in the attacks. Most likely I think she was because no woman could kill six or so soldiers in a few minutes without someone noticing something. And the odd thing was the guards didn't even know what took place. They were still at their post doing what they were supposed to do and that was to stand fast and keep and look out. Well, in the morning while they were breaking down camp, the lieutenant noticed that some of the tents were not being broken down and that no one answered when the lieutenant called out to the tents. And when they entered the tents, they saw dead men whose necks had marks on them.

And as they felt them, those whom had the marks on their necks were cold and presumed that they had died. So they proceeded to bury them and as they looked around, they went and shook the woman's tent and she was gone. So at first they figured that an animal such as a viper had attacked the men in their tents and the woman had perhaps been attacked and forced to go with whoever it was that threatened her on the path. So Humood ordered his men to bury the fallen among them and to begin to search the area for the woman and see if she was in danger or if she had just walked off and was trying to get home. But either way, he wanted to question her about if she had seen or heard anything that night. Humood then told the king and I that as they finished up the camp and burials that they set off in two directions, and remember, he originally was leading a group of a little more than a hundred men, he and his men never found the woman, so they left off searching for her.

And as they had done the night before, they began to set up their tents for some rest and food from their day's travels. He stated that they were about twenty miles away from where the first incident had taken place and that they had done all they could to set up guards and make sure the encampment was safe. During the night, a guard challenged a small group of men that began to approach the camp. The guard yelled, 'Alarm! Alert! Wake up! Wake up! Stations!' And the camp began to rise up and prepare to meet whatever threat was coming. Well, as the guards began to prepare themselves to meet the challengers that approached them, suddenly they heard a voice say, 'No alarm, no fear. It's us, your comrades. You left us behind.' As the camp rushed out to form, a guard went down to confirm what was being said by whom and he was carrying a torch and suddenly, the torch was darkened and all the others heard was a scream. So Humood said that he and his men formed up and began to light torches and began to spread out in groups of ten to see who was there. He then said that they came upon the body of their fallen guard and that his neck was torn out. And he blew his horn and the men were ordered to regroup and reform back in the camp. And when they got to the camp, they saw the six comrades drinking what seemed to be the blood of a fallen horse that they must have killed. As soon as Humood said he saw those men and that they were thought to have been dead but now are not, he said that he asked them what happened and why have they killed one of our horses and are drinking the blood that is against the law? He said one answered and said, 'Law? We are above the law. Join us and we can start our own kingdom. A kingdom of will where whatever we will, we will do.'

Humood asked them if they killed Moustop or tore out his throat. One of the six answered and said, 'What if we did? He threatened us and I wasn't in the mood to tolerate his questions.' Humood then said that he began to approach the men and ordered them to be arrested and taken back to the barracks for trial for murder of a fellow soldier and the killing and drinking of the blood of a horse. All of the sudden, the men rushed them with the speed of a bear in full charge knocking several soldiers down and tossing others out of their way as though they were just mere rag dolls. He said that a few of those men were set upon by the ones that were following the first ones that lead the attack. So as those men were being devoured by the ones behind, the others began to charge towards the main body of men. Humood said that he ordered the men to quickly get in order and some began to shoot arrows at the beast men, but it only stopped them for a few moments as they stopped to pull out the arrows from their bodies. He then stated that as some of these beast men broke upon them, that they began to pull man by man out of the ranks and throw them down to the ground where the three following would try and hold them down and tear out their necks or bite them in some fashion like a serpent. He then stated that as one of his men shot an arrow, that it hit one in the chest around the heart and that the beast man stopped cold, fell to the ground and did not get up, so he started to order those that were shooting arrows to aim for the chest which is also the heart area so to try to stop the beast men. Again, remember, we don't know if that stopped the beast men or if it was because their being hit by so many arrows that they lost blood and that is why they were trying to drink the other men's blood in a vain effort to replenish their own lost blood. So as the fighting and dying continued, Humood said he was now facing one of these beast men and that it was coming for him and he stabbed the man in the stomach and the man's insides fell out on the ground.

He said the man just looked at him and laughed and that his insides started to rise back into the man's stomach and he was beginning to heal right in front of him. And while the man laughed, Humood looked at the man and said, "I will smite you evil demon in the name of God," and took off the man's head. He fell over dead and he didn't heal or recover from that blow. As Humood prepared himself for his next opponent, he noticed that the one hit with an arrow in the chest and in the heart also didn't move or rise or heal from his wounds. And it was apparently noticed as well by the beast men as Humood called them because after Humood had beheaded one of the beast men in battle, then the others suddenly had begun to run away. Humood ordered all of his men to keep firing arrows at them until they were no longer able to be seen in the darkness. And remember this, my men, Humood lost that night twenty-five more men in just two nights. He had lost a total of thirty-one men, almost a third of his men to a small group of vipers and a small group of his own men.

Humood told us that seeing what had happened to his men was painful, but he ordered as a precaution that any man who had been taken down by the beast men to be burnt by fire to purify their bodies before God and to bring their souls to rest. He also ordered that the one taken down by arrows was to be beheaded and then burnt by fire as well.

He then set up watch all night for the men and told them to rotate in sleep and watch that they might hunt down their attackers from the night before."

Clive spoke up and said, "Trist, are you making this up? I mean, it is a good story, but it's just a tale to scare small children, right?" Trist answered and said, "No Clive, Humood wrote a daily journal and he spent all day and night copying it so that our kingdom would have a copy and he did this if we agreed to pass the word along to the other kingdoms about what happened to us and them during their journeys. So we agreed and I'm passing it on to you here so you might remember how to possibly stop these beast men if anymore exist. But remember, not a word leaves this troop! Keep your mouths shut and your eyes opened for trouble." And the men all stomped and said, "Yes, sir!"

Trist continued on and said, "Humood went out the next day and found nothing. And then the next day and again found nothing. Then on the third day of their search, they found the four remaining men with a wolf hanging in a tree upside down and they were draining the blood of the animal into a pan of some kind and were dipping their fingers into the pan and placing them each one into their mouths. He ordered the men to charge these beasts upon their horses and to strike their necks. The men did charge and one of the beasts was slashed down almost immediately because while he was drinking the blood, it seemed to Humood that the man was in some sort of trance from the effects of the blood. But the other three began to run like bears and Humood and his men followed them. He said that they lost them for a few moments but that one of their trackers picked up their trails and then they followed them to a small cave. They knew the men were inside because Humood and his men could easily hear them talking and moving in the cave. It was quite clear they were going deeper inside the cave and wanted him and his men to follow them. So Humood left ten men to guard their stuff and took the remaining fifty-nine men armed with spears, swords and torches. As he and his men proceeded inside the cave, they began to hear voices all around them. They also began to hear water running and they began to have several small rocks being thrown at them as to taunt them into coming ever deeper inside the cave. Humood and his men slowly progressed into the cave and then they had to decide whether or not to venture into the small creek that was forming in the interior of the cave. So he ordered his men to push on and keep watching as they began to mark their paths so that they could trace a way back out of the cave. Because what they had thought was but a small cave opening turned out to be a very nice sized cave. Suddenly, they followed the voices to a path in the cave that went up a small distance and seemed to be the head of a small underground waterfall that was only a few dozen paces across and only about as deep as the thighs of a man's waist. So he and his men proceeded to move on up the small path one by one until they reached the top of the falls. There on the top was nothing but echoes. Just echoes that seemed to get louder and louder. Mocking them to come and fight, taunting them to hasten to their deaths and become the food of their gods. So Humood urged his men ever forward seeking out their query and they came to a point on the top of the ledge that they either had to go back or cross the small creek where the waterfall fell from. So Humood told his men that the water is not too swift and to let them take their time and cross over through the middle and proceed to follow in the water up to that shore over where they can get back on dry cave rock and follow the voices and kill those bastards.

So, he and his men proceeded to jump into the creek with their gear being ever mindful to keep their torches dry so they could see with what little light there was and as the last man got into the water, suddenly one of the man beasts ran at them again with the speed of a wild animal from the other side coming out of the darkness into the light just long enough to get their attention. He leaped up into the air crashing into a dozen men and as these men were hit by the force of the man beast, they dropped their weapons and fell into the water with their dozen torches being submerged in the attack. The other men behind them began to form up in the water to advance to aid their brothers in arms, but suddenly two men began to be dragged backwards as swift as the current could carry them but apparently there was a force helping drag them backwards because the current was fast but not that strong. Then next the men saw that what was in the back was their friends being lifted up by two beast men as they arose up out of the water with the men held high in their arms and tossed them to the cave floor below to their deaths. Then the men began to form up in groups and the front proceeded to move forward to help give light to their friends that had been hit by a beast man lunging at them from the cave floor to the creek and the back group formed up with Humood to take and deal with the two that had dragged their friends to the falls and threw them to their deaths.

As suddenly as this all was taking place, the fourth beast man jumped up from the middle of the creek and grabbed a man and tore out his neck and the water began to fill with blood. Many of the men began to panic because they seemed to be everywhere and the light was going out or flickering and it was getting harder and harder to see because torches were being lost in the water as the fighting was going on.

Humood said that he ordered his men in the back where they were to stay strong and yell at the men in front to fight and for the men in the center to try and help them. One of the men with

Humood brought his arrow and he raised it and shot at one of the beast men by the falls and hit him in his head and the beast man turned and pulled the arrow out of his head and began to run at them in the creek fighting the current while the other beast man dove back into the water and began to swim in up to us as fast as a fish. The man with his arrow shot again and this time he hit the beast man in the heart and the man fell backwards and didn't move and the current took him over the edges of the falls. But while this was happening, suddenly the beast man in the middle apparently doubled back from the center underwater and pulled Humood under. Quickly one of Humood's men slashed at the beast man barely missing Humood and striking off the beast man's arm and the beast man let out a harrowing scream that filled the cave with echoes. The beast man let go and another of Humood's men grabbed him and helped to drag him out of the water. As the beast man began to run back, he was grabbed by two soldiers and stabbed in the back and in the neck. And a couple more men then assisted the men and tossed him back to the cave floor and hurried and beheaded the creature. During that time, the beast man that swam up the creek to the men leapt up and grabbed two soldiers by their helmets and crushed their heads together like two eggs. He then proceeded to go back underwater while the men were in disarray and proceeded to bite one's leg which caused the man to fall down and be carried over the falls. Then he grabbed another man by the waist and proceeded to pull him down, but suddenly the men began to jab their spears and swords in and out of the water in unison in an effort to make their submerged attacker leave or surface. It worked! The beast man was hit several times and the water continued to get bloodier by the minute so the beast man jumped up out of the water and ran quickly to the other side of the cave and dashed to the darkness further back in the cave's interior.

Meanwhile, the men in the front formation had been knocked down, but other than that escaped any major harm. They made all due effort to slash, stab and poke the water to see if they could provoke an attack from the beast that just slammed into them but to no avail. He couldn't be found.

So Humood ordered the men to quickly form up and cross the creek and to proceed to track down the wounded beast man first because he was leaving a large trail of blood and entrails. So as he and his men followed the beast man, they then found him slumping over a small rock as though he was waiting for them. He looked up and said, "I will eat you all when I finish healing up."

Humood ordered his men to charge as best they could over the slippery cave floor. Many of his men were falling down and some were stumbling around because they couldn't see very well due to a lack of lighting from the torches that remained. And as the men attacked, the wounded beast man suddenly jumps out from behind a crevasse in the cave floor and grabbed two men and pulled their heads down underneath his armpits and he broke their necks. The men began to slash at these two beasts and the wounded beast slashed with his one good arm taking out two more soldiers' throats but finally he was pinned to the wall of the cave with a spear and another soldier came up and slashed off his head in one fell swoop of the sword. The other beast man was jumping, slashing, kicking and fighting as a wild dragon. But he also was finally dispatched by the use of spears taking out one of his legs long enough for another spear to pierce his chest and go through to his heart, but after all this, Humood said he also ordered the men to take off this creature's head as well. So they then gathered up the bodies of all of the fallen and the beast men that they could find and proceeded out of the cave to their guard detail. All the bodies were burnt and to be safe, each one was beheaded to prevent further infection.

Through all of this, Humood lost thirty-eight of his men and he sent some back to give a report and kept a few with him. But this again is but one of his reports that we have a copy of to his king. I don't have time to tell you about the other stories he has written about nor do I want to. I personally read his report about four times since we first received it so that I could understand each and every nuisance of what had happened and what we were facing. I felt I owed that much to Humboldt and the men that we lost on this journey.

So, does everyone understand the dangers we now may face?"

All of the men replied, "Yes, sir!"

After all of this time, Drang stood in silence taking mental notes as to what was being said. Drang was the quiet type, but he was a solid young man that would have rather done anything than join the King's army. He had hopes and dreams of his own, but at least for now those hopes and dreams were on hold...or were they?

CHAPTER 5

I finally arrive.
As Drang stood still listening to the words that were being spoken as the men of the troop continued to linger around after they had been dismissed, he silently but intently listened to the gossip and hearsay that had already crept into the castle since the king and his men had arrived back from their scouting trip.

Drang was much more interested in studying with some of the local inventors and men of science and words than worrying about some mere sickness that was taking hold upon the land. Besides, how many other illnesses in times past had come and gone? We've faced the plague, cold, heat, drought and storms of all types and yet here we are and Satu Mare is still here and as far as I'm concerned will always be here until the Lord takes this place for Himself. Drang continued to think to himself, 'I don't want this promotion to second. This is not my life-long goal and besides, it will only cause me problems. There are many others here that have been near lifers and they should have this position way before I because when this trouble is over, all I want to do is go back home and see what I can learn and what mysterious wonders this land holds. I want to explore from the plains to the rivers and back again and maybe to the oceans which are afar for now and maybe I could work on a ship for a few years and then come back and tell all of the ladies

I was a great adventurer. That's what I want to do.' Drang then briskly began to walk towards the cathedral where services for the fallen were being held.

While I looked at myself in the mirror, I thought, 'Why am I always brushed off by Father and Mother? When will they treat me like a regent in waiting? I should be informed about all that is taking place in the kingdom especially since Father was going out on patrols with his men as of late. What if something happened to him and he never came back? Then I would be the second to the throne and God forbid but if something then happened to Mother, perhaps she was taken by this maddening sickness, then what? How could I take the reins of power without knowing what is facing the kingdom and for that matter, it may take the kingdom awhile to get used to the loss of Humboldt?

Trist will have to find his royal footing in the kingdom and around here that can take quite a lot of work. I mean Trist is a far younger man than Humboldt was. Humboldt was in his late forties and maybe even fifty, but Trist is but a mere twenty-seven years old and that is a far cry to Humboldt's age and experience. Father and Mother will also have to adjust to Trist and his advice as will Father Millinus because Trist is less reserved than Humboldt was.

Humboldt was thoughtful and yet sharp. He could speak to one without speaking a word and when he did speak, then everyone knew to be quiet and take heed to what he thought and was saying because he had been around and seen alot. I guess that is what we will all miss the most about Humboldt not being around anymore. His great wisdom and warming personality.' I finished wiping the tears from my eyes.

'Oh, now look what you've done,' I thought. 'Now I have to have Mercia come and help me wash my face and readjust my blush and powder. Oh, you silly, silly girl! Why can't you be more like Mother and keep things inside and only let them out when no one is around?' I then began to rise up after having had Mercia help me remove and redo my facial powder. I began to drift slowly around my room and asked Mercia about her day and if she had anything that she was going to do in the evening.

"Well, I don't know about anyone else, but I'm going to the courtyard this evening to enjoy the celebration that is being put on for the men that have come back from this successful journey. I plan to dance and sway the night away until I can't stand on my feet anymore." I said. "Where is Justarly?" Mercia reminded me that he was escorting my Mother around the courtyard helping to make sure everything was in order or being set in place for the next few nights' celebration. I responded, "Oh, thank you Mercia. Now go and fetch me Catherine, Elia and Miranda so we can figure out which gowns we should wear. I so want us to match up perfectly and I want everything to be just right because all of the young men will be out tonight in their dress uniforms. They always look so nice in their outfits and I want us to aim to please and of course I hope all eyes are upon me. Oh, and please remind Myra and Vilian not to goof around tonight.

I want to be the light in the night sky and if they blow this for me, then my wrath will be horrible. My sisters can be quite the pranksters at times but sometimes they don't know when to quit and if they do anything that makes me a mocking or laughing point to the people, then I hope they are ready because even Mother won't be able to save them if they do. And oh, tell Catherine to please not flaunt her abundant bosoms. I would like to have a few of the men's eyes looking in our faces tonight and not just at our perks."

As I began to finish up scouting about my room and going from closet to closet comparing gown after gown and shoe after shoe, I threw them down on the bed for a possible choice or back in another closet for a 'not at all chance I'm going to wear you tonight.' I drifted back in front of the mirror and looked and said, "What to wear, what to wear and what will make me look really nice this evening." Pushing up my breasts while I gently tugged on them, I said, "Oh, I wish they were bigger. But I've got a butt to die for. If only I was the perfect woman with the whole kit. The perfect looks, hair, breasts and body. Oh so close, but yet so far away."

In the meantime, girls began to come into my room one by one starting with of course Myra and Vilian, my two younger sisters. I yelled, "What are you doing in my room? The celebration is several hours away and I want to get ready without distractions."

Myra said, "Sunny, we are just wanting to come in and use your mirror to look at ourselves because your mirror is so big and ours is so much smaller. Besides, you always look so nice that we want to look like you, right Vilian?" Vilian nodded intently while looking at some of the gowns I had tossed upon the bed.

Vilian who was ever curious said, "Sahnedra, why do you hate us?" I replied, "I don't hate you, you just get in the way and mess up almost everything I want to do. Every time I try and talk to Mother or Father, you seem to go out of your way and distract them so they ignore what I'm trying to get across to them and that is why I like being away from you two so much." Myra reacted, "That's just plain rude! You say all that, but you seem to forget that most of the time you get into trouble by your choices and might I add that many of them are almost always bad. I mean, here you are our elder sister and you treat me like a baby. I'm seventeen years old and Vilian is fifteen years of age. You should include us in your events and plans and as equals with your friends. But no, you ignore us and the only time we get any attention from you is if we pull a joke on you. Why can't you invite us to go down with you in your carriage tonight with you and your friends to the great Ball party? Why does big boobed Catherine get to come in here or Elia and to make matters worse even Miranda is included? Even she gets to come in here and dress with you and compare gowns, shoes and necklaces. Why not us? We're your sisters, dammit!"

At that Mercia chimed in and said, "Watch your cursing mouth right now little princess or I will talk to your Mother and Father

Millinus about your use of such drib! Ladies, don't speak such in the presence of royalty or others whom they respect, and to be frank with you, it's not proper words for a Christian to speak before the Lord.

So, get ready or be off with you and do what it is you do, but let us get it done so you girls can go out and have a good time."

Myra, having seen she was bluntly rebuked, replied, "Yes, ma'am, you're right. I should watch my words better, but Sahnedra just makes me so mad. I feel like I could eat horseshoes." All the while I was snickering to the grimaces of Myra and Vilian, Mercia spoke up and said, "Sahnedra, if I had such fine sisters as these, I would be proud to include them in all of my affairs. Good friends are hard to find but good sisters are even harder. Let them join you and your friends for Mercia's sake. How about if they promise to behave and not make any scenes tonight or do anything that might upset you and embarrass you or your friends? What do you say?" I looked with a frown upon my face and a smirk and said, "Only if they promise not to stand above us this year and pour water down our tops. And no crawling under the table and trying to attach a string to Elia's petticoat. Oh yes, and the ever famous tart joke where they tossed from the ledge hot tarts at me and Miranda's backsides. They also need to stop pulling at Catherine's hair and trying to grab the slit in between her breasts so that they are exposed to the whole country side. If they can do that, then I might consider it."

Vilian said, "I agree. We won't pull any tricks on you or your friends this time if you let us go and besides, you got us back and that wasn't funny either." I stated, "Yes, but my revenge was in private, but so help me if you bother me in even the slightest way this year, then you will see what it's like to have your pricklies shown to the whole country. Understood? It's no fun having your backsides exposed before the whole court because some little brats don't understand that they are too young to do what those of us that have reached womanhood can do." Myra chimed in, "Well, with those small to mid-nubs you call boobs; I'm surprised you were ashamed at all when your top fell down a few years ago. You are almost as flat as a young boy. I mean, you couldn't give suck to a small cat let alone a man." Vilian also piped in while laughing, "Or even a small baby! Oh, I've got to stop laughing! Stop it Myra! I think I might have to pee. Ha, ha...ah....I feel sick!"

I stared and then stated, "Do you see? This is why I can't stand you guys and this is why my friends literally hate you! You're babies and you're jealous of our looks and those that look at us! And I will have you know I could give suck to a small cat and for that matter if you two ever get boyfriends which may be impossible with that ugly blonde hair, Myra! And Vilian being the ginger of the ages, well, I could give suck to both of your men at one time if you had any and when they were done to whoever else wanted a peaking taste of these fine breasts from God."

And with that, Mercia entered the room and said, "Are we agreed then? Have you fine daughters of King Dargon decided to finally work together and have a blessed time?" And all the girls looked at each other and smiled, but I with a small hint of sarcasm turned and said, "Yes, Mercia, we will all try and get together and work out our differences." As Mercia left the room smiling thinking she had averted a royal crisis, I ran and shut the door behind Mercia as she exited the room and then leapt over a group of shoes and quickly but quietly grabbed Myra and Vilian by the necks and pulled them so close to me that the three's noses were touching each others. I then proceeded to say, "If you do anything to make me look bad in front of our royal house and the guests that will arrive here from Russia, then I will cut your off your nipples and give them to the cats on the street or hand them out as pacifiers for toddlers to suck on. Do I make myself clear?"

Myra grabbed my hand and tossed it away and said, "Yes, I get it. You'll kill us, right?" I replied, "Right. Vilian, how about you?" Vilian said, "I get it, but you really grabbed me hard and my neck hurts now, and oh, your breath stinks. You might want to do something about that since your girlfriends will be arriving anytime now."

I responded and said, "Okay, then you can come and I'm sorry I grabbed your neck so hard, but you need to toughen up some. You're weak and always have been a cry baby, and oh, thanks for telling me about my breath. With all the excitement that has been going on since Father came home and the death of Humboldt and the others, I haven't eaten all day and now I probably won't eat until tonight, but no matter. We will have plenty of food soon. Come on, let's get my friends and let's all get undressed when they arrive so that we can all dress to slay whoever looks at us."

Suddenly, a small group of three knocks tapped upon the entrance of the door. I asked, "Who is it?" Behind the large door came a sharp but high pitched voice, "It's me and the girls, Sahnedra. Can we come in? We tried, but for some reason the door is locked." Vilian got up off of the floor with a bounce and unlocked the door. And with a click of the lock, the three girls Catherine, Elia and the ever lovely Miranda pranced into the room each with an arm full of dresses and a few ladies behind them with a sack or so full of shoes.

Catherine bragged, "I just got this lovely blue dress for you all to see it. I love how it shows off all my bounty, if you know what I mean girls." Elia giggled, "I bet it does." Miranda chimed in, "Yeah, I guess you don't want to make them wonder what's under that top. Ha! Ha! You sure do love to show your crevasse."

Catherine replied, "Well, why not? If you got it, then one should use it to one's advantage. I don't want to end up with some old balding man for a husband now do I?" "And what about you?" I asked, "What are you going to wear Elia and Miranda? I bet you both have some beautiful treasures to show me as well."

Elia answered, "Oh, let me go first! Look at my slippers! Aren't they perfect? They are all silver. My gown is laced in silver with a gold trim top. My gown should sparkle in the moonlight and should reflect the firelight as well. I plan to turn the heads of some young handsome men in my direction tonight."

Miranda slowly grabbed a gown and with her back turned to her friends, pulled it up to her neckline and then slowly turned around. Suddenly all of the girls in the room screamed with excitement and they all were saying, "That is beautiful! Who made it for you? Oh, we want one! Can we trade for it?"

Miranda smiled, "This is all mine, girls. It is sheer silk with gold woven in with crushed blue dye oysters added in the mix and I have a scarf with rubies that will sit around my neck and a headdress to go on my head that is layered in pure silver. My dress is a perfect mix of blue oyster dye and silk with gold inlay." All the girls gasped and said in unison, "Yes, it's so lovely just like you! No wonder they call you 'yummy'. Everything you wear looks so good that all the men want to marry you and when they get done tasting the food you bring to the celebration, they always say that yours is the yummiest." I complimented, "Oh, Miranda, you're the perfect woman! You can cook, you can dress and you're just beautiful! God has truly blessed you."

Miranda replied, "He didn't do a bad job on the rest of you either. I mean, look at you guys! After we get dressed up today, then we women will be the closest things to fallen angels these men will ever see in their lifetimes." While the girls laughed, they continued to undress and try on various undergarments aiding one another as they needed it. And then they proceeded to try and exchange shoes, tops, and bottoms each just looking for that perfect fit. And of course each one trying to outdo the others. Finally, each one arrived at just the right match in regards to what they wanted to wear to show the world that night. Each girl looked lovely and bristled with vibrance and life. They appeared in their own way to be a woman in waiting. Young, strong, fertile and yes, waiting for that man that would one day take her to himself that they might rule their own families together.

Myra, Vilian and I all agreed to try and look alike so as to complement each other's outfits and to somewhat stand apart for the other girls lovely gowns. Because tonight they had a special guest that would arrive from the furthest reaches of the borders. To land until now was told to them as children in stories, but in fact the stories must be true because tonight a princess was coming to join them to talk trade and diplomacy with Father and Mother over the next week or so after the celebration of the return of our men back home had ended. These things usually lasted for a few days until the food ran low and the wine, ale and other assorted hard spirits ran low or out.

But Myra, Vilian and my gowns simmered in the light of the sun and it was hoped they would do so by the light of the moon, candles and fires. We each had a small crown with one small red ruby in the center top, and upon our necks lay some of the elaborate hand worked gold necklaces the kingdom could produce. Then the gowns were all what Satu Mare would call 'angel's feathers.' These are gowns that are white silk and lace tapered together with interwoven rotating bands of fine silver and gold and all this proceeds down to the ankles. The slippers were hand-woven, but sturdily soft, hand-woven silk and a hint of green gems going down the sides of the slippers. Finally, the girls were ready to present themselves before the king and then before the people.

While Dargon was making sure that everything was in order, he ventured to and fro seeking council with Father Millinus concerning the state of the ill Ralisu who had been attacked and bitten by the beast people of the journey. He sought out Trist and Justarly for concerns dealing with security and the keeping of the watch during the celebrations. He talked to the keepers of the castle about having rooms ready to receive the princess from Russia.

Everything was going as planned and then she arrived. A voice could be heard from the city and fires were being lit and trumpets began to sound as the princess from the East Country and her carriage with her escort in the lead climbed its way to the castle through the city's streets. With all the noise that was taking place, my girlfriends and I rushed to the window to see the carriage that was carrying this supposed lovely but as yet hidden and mysterious princess.

Who was she and what was she like? How was Russia? Were they really as powerful as everyone claimed? What language did she speak and what color was she? All these questions had raced around in my head and my friends and sisters heads as well.

The excitement was building and I began to hope that maybe someday I would be allowed to travel with the princess quite possibly back to Russia and that maybe she could be the kingdom trade envoy. Yes, the small kingdom of Satu Mare might be able to become more powerful if only they could develop trade relations with this new and exciting kingdom.

So I looked quickly at her sisters and said, "Girls, grab them by the hands and everyone be careful, but let's be quick. Let's run, but don't appear to be too hasty that we can stand beside Father and Mother and all the court so we can present ourselves as princesses and nobles to this newly arrived ambassador that she might accept us as her friends and equals."

So we all hurriedly raced through the halls and swept down the stairs and at a brisk pace we finally arrived hand in hand with Father and Mother and the whole court being present at the front gate of the castle. We all anxiously waited for the carriage of the princess to arrive. As quickly as the girls and everyone else present were making sure that they were groomed and proper to receive such an honored guest, then the carriage began to crest the hill being led by six men on white horses and trailed by six wagons each carrying two more men each and yet they were themselves being followed by six more men on black horses.

"Oh, what a parade," I thought, "I hope one day to be able to be in one such as this and be able to represent my Father in important matters of the court."

Suddenly the carriage arrived and pulled up and stopped. The men on the wagons, horses and the carriage got off and stood in equal numbers per say on both sides of the carriage door. Father beckoned and four men began to unroll a red carpet that was trimmed in gold that was trimmed in silver edges with bronze tassels at the ends of it. This carpet was unrolled from the entrance of the gate of the castle to the first step stool that was set up for the princess so that the first thing her feet would touch before she touched the ground was the royal purple stool. This was the custom in those days and it showed that we accepted the guests as a royal and that while she was in our kingdom, she would have the same right and privileges as any other royal. She also by default became a temporary member of our family and would be shown the same courtesies that we ourselves received from the court's servants.

As the men hurriedly unfurled the red carpet and set up the purple royal stool below the last rung of the carriage steps, Father beckoned Trist and Justarly to proceed in formation up the red carpet to open the door and the other to place out their hand that the princess might grab it to use it to steady herself to the ground. Father and Mother proceeded after them so that they could be the first to welcome the princess to our kingdom followed by Father Millinus and a few other priests from the Order of High Palin. These would offer a blessing upon the princess right after she has received welcome from Father and Mother as well as a few words of high praise concerning the great tales about what has been said about her land of origin.

Then my sisters and I and all of the other nobles would wait until Father and Mother led the princess back to us that they may introduce each one of us in person by name to the princess. Then the servants would bow, gather her things and proceed to quarter her escorts, feed the horses, wash the carriage and then return to normal events in preparation for the night's festivities.

The opening of the carriage lingered for a moment and it was now getting toward the dusk of the evening with the sun preparing to set. Suddenly, the door opened and we anxiously waited to see who and what we would receive into our kingdom. Be it good or bad.

CHAPTER 6

The ball begins.

As the darkness quickly began to descend upon us at the gathering, I could see a long, slender leg peek out from the carriage door. And then there came out a beautiful young lady who was tall and thin with blond hair flowing down her back. She gracefully seemed to glide down the steps of the carriage one by one gently reaching out for the hands of Trist and his assistant.

The princess of Russia came over very quietly but yet in a royal, regal manner to where our whole court was lined up to meet and greet her highness. She began by introducing herself as Nathisa, princess of Russia as she bowed slightly. And of course, Father began to introduce himself as he bent over to kiss her hand. He then proceeded to introduce my Mother and bows were exchanged and so on it went until they arrived at me.

Father introduced me and spoke very highly of me and my sisters and the rest of the court and asked if I would be willing to show the princess to her room. I of course responded, "Yes, I will gladly escort her." So as we went, I said, "Nathisa, will you be joining us for the festival tonight?" She replied, "But of course. That is why I waited to exit the carriage because I was putting on the finishing touches to my outfit. I wanted to look very good for you all this evening." She continued, "Do you have any Russian

Blues cats in the castle? Because if not, then I will have my Father send you a few so you can see how wonderful they are to have as pets and besides, they bring good luck to any kingdom. And I think from what I'm hearing, you and your kingdom are in need of a little good luck right now."

I responded, "What makes you think that we are in need of good luck? We don't have any Russian Blue cats at this moment, but if you can, I would love one and please give me one for Catherine. She is a big cat lover."

Nathisa commented, "Well, I meant no offense, but there's so many rumors of strange attacks going on in all the surrounding kingdoms, and I've seen hundreds of men going up and down the roadways as if they are searching or patrolling the whole kingdom almost as if you are at war, but I know you are not because I wouldn't have been allowed to make this trip if such were the case." I replied, "No, we are not at war and you are right. We have had a few strange happenings over the last few months, and in fact, that is why we are having this festival tonight because Father and many of his men came back and concluded a special trip to secure a faraway area of our countryside. But we are playing it safe and keeping our guard up just in case something else might seek to pop up its evil head."

As Nathisa and I rounded the corner of the inner castle, we both had passed a quick moving Father Millinus. He quickly waved at them and spoke in a hurried manner, almost rambling as he moved past them. "Excuse me girls, but I have to get to the room with Ralisu and check on him. They say his fever is breaking. I think we may have beaten this thing." He bowed slightly while still moving, "Enjoy the festival and I hope to see you both there. We all deserve it after what we have endured over the last few days."

Nathisa just smiled at me and gently grabbed me by my hand and said, "I hope you don't think this bad of me, but would you allow me to shadow you tonight? Because I know no one and am all alone and besides you, I don't know who to speak to." I replied, "No, that is fine. I sort of expected you to grace me with your presence. Besides, with you around, I'm sure all the young men will come by and seek our hands for a dance or two." We both continued to walk down to the corridor until we reached my room. Her things had already been brought to the room by the court's servants and so all she had to do was open the door and all her needs would be met from that point forward. Nathisa exclaimed, "I will do a quick touch up and then I will meet you down the hallway and we can all go to the ball together, yes?" I replied with a smile and a nod.

Justarly was walking the grounds and making sure security of the castle walls were complete and in order and then he dispatched some of the queen's guards to go and make sure that the completed area would house the festival that was also under adequate guard as well. He thought to himself, 'Nothing must go wrong tonight. Nothing must be allowed to go wrong tonight. Should I increase the number of men around the area? Should I send out extra patrols and increase the checkpoints? Surely not. But what if I'm wrong? And as he was walking around and checking out all points of view on paper and in person, Buddy ran up to him and barked at him. He then proceeded to nip at his uniform and then continued to bark at him. Justarly looked down and said, "Oh, hi Buddy. What's going on with you? Do you want some attention or just another piece of meat from the butcher's shop?" Justarly reached down and rubbed Buddy on the head and he poked him in the nose and said, "That's a good dog. Now be off with you and go and find Sahnedra and her troop and make sure they are safe." Buddy looked up at him as if to say thanks for your time and sniffed and proceeded to go and run up towards the last general direction where I and my friends had been.

Well at long last, the festival was beginning and the whole countryside seemed to be in attendance. Uniforms were everywhere. Glorious dresses and gowns were flowing down and up as men and women proceeded to dance and drink and feast like there was no tomorrow. The Order of Palin was out handing out apples and various other kinds of fruits to the poor and homeless as many orphaned children were examined for any signs of unusual coloration of the skin or weird body markings. Yes, that was the Order of Palin seeking to work even when fun was all around them. Father Millinus called them an Order within an Order of do-gooders that can't do well enough because there is never enough good in the world.

Myra and Vilian were already at the festival staring down at the great assembly from a small, yet perched up hillside that gave them the advantage to see everything almost at once because they didn't want to miss a thing. Catherine, Elia and Miranda were already eating and talking to the young men around them, but they were all waiting to see me arrive with the newest girl in the group. Princess Nathisa. Their arrival would be the crowning moment of the night's events because it was expected that the young royals make a slightly later appearance than everyone else because they had to shine like the moon in the night's sky. It was expected that they would be asked to dance with some of the finest men in the kingdom and any other visiting guests to the festival that were from the various far flung kingdoms adjacent to their own. A few minutes later coming down the main walkway for all to see was two gorgeously dressed young women both of which were wearing almost the same matching gowns. These gowns fit very closely to their slender bodies and stuck out in all the right places accenting what needed to be accented. Their hair was all braided with gold and silver inlays and their shoes seemed to shimmer in the light of the fire and starlight above. Yes, they were a sight for all to behold, but who all was beholding them?

Nathisa and I joined up with all the girls and began to speak to one another concerning different topics and they all seemed to be enjoying each other's company. Suddenly a trumpet began to blow and the festival began to settle down. It was the official beginning of the festival that always started out with the royal couple having the first dance together in the center of the dance area. As they proceeded to dance, the various men of the court began to ask their wives or girlfriends or some other lady in waiting to dance with them until everyone that was of like mind joined in for the festival of fun.

The evening went on and on and dancing continued, but eating and drinking were just as important as dancing. In some areas, magic was being performed and in others, various games of chance were taking place. In some areas, cards were being played and yet in other places, people were just sitting and talking to one another. 'All in all, this is a lovely night.' I thought to myself. 'I wonder where I will meet him? The one that will make my heart skip a beat and at the same time beat like the heart of a young baby rabbit. Where will he be and what will he look like?' Nathisa grabbing Catherine by the hand said, "Come with me! I will dance with you and we will have fun." Catherine agreed and they proceeded to dance and twirl and spin each other around all the while they laughed and the young men all gathered around. Several other young ladies joined in and began to sing along with one another. The young men formed a circle around the young ladies as they danced and sang and they began to clap and dance on the outside of the dance area and joined in the singing.

I was drinking a glass of wine as I smiled and continued to watch all the frivolities that were taking place around me. I thought to myself, 'I wonder if he is here? And where is Father Millinus? I see a lot of the other priests around doing the works of the Order and yes, taking part in the eating and drinking and I do believe that some of them are debating the Scriptures, but where is Father Millinus? If he misses this festival, that would be such a shame. It's so beautiful outside. I'd like to ask him to dance with me so he could tell me how beautiful I am and how he loves my new gown.

Maybe I should go and look for him or no, he said he was checking on Ralisu. Wow! What a sickness that must be! It's been days and he still isn't up from his bed. I hope everything is getting better for him because he would like this festival as well and who knows I might dance with him if he asks me to.'

Father Millinus was busy, much too busy to think about any festival. The fever that had taken hold of Ralisu was gone, but yet the bite marks seemed to be worse. Father Millinus instructed some of the priests to go and heat an iron and get some wine or alcohol so that he might treat the apparent infectious wounds that were on Ralisu's body. Ralisu said, "Father, it is ok. I'm fine. Let's go to the festival right now. We can deal with these scars later." Father Millinus replied, "No my son. I must burn the scars out and make sure they are not infectious on you or anyone else. We must take every precaution that it will not come back and that you won't die from anything such as gangrene or pus or anything else that might be a part of this plague. I pray to God that you are cured and not able to get this plague. Maybe God has made you above it." Father Millinus proceeded to apply the hot iron to the wounded infected areas and as Ralisu screamed from the pain that was caused, Father Millinus prayed as he worked for Ralisu to be healed of any infectious demonic plague that might seek to invade the young man's body. After the application of the hot iron to Ralisu, he eventually passed out from the extreme pain that was caused and the shock his system was under. Father Millinus spoke to the priest of his order and instructed them to keep close watch upon the young man for any signs of a change either good or bad and no matter what, to keep him informed and to give him limited freedom of movement. But he must not be allowed to mingle at this time with any other persons but the Order. And this was done to limit the chance of exposing others to the demonic beast man plague.

Father Millinus proceeded to wipe off his brow outside with a small rag and from a fresh cool bucket of water that one of the priests had fetched and brought to him. I walked over and said, "There you are! Do you want to come join me for the festival? We haven't had our dance yet." Father Millinus smiled and replied, "You know I would love to dance with you, but I'm not as dressed up because I've been busy helping our wounded soldier, but if you can stand the sight of me, then I'm yours for a couple of dances." I smiled and with a wink and a nod, I proceeded to grab him by his hand and pulled him close to me and escorted him proudly to the dancing area of the festival. Along the way, Father Millinus couldn't help but grab an apple and a bit of free brewed beer to wash it down with. Of course, the beer was brewed by his order just for such an occasion as this. I watched him finish off his drink and asked, "Are you ready now?" Father Millinus replied, "Yes child, I'm always ready. By the way, the reason I love the Order's brew so much better than the common brew is because it doesn't contain alcohol like the common so I can drink all I want and quench my thirst but yet still dance and play like the best of them. Ha...ah...ah."

Father Millinus proceeded to do his traditional bow and held out his hand and said, "Madam, may I ask your hand for this dance?" I didn't say a word. Grabbing Father Millinus's hand, I rounded up in a twirl and proceeded to allow him to lead me in the dance. I thought to myself, 'Millinus isn't married or has a wife. He would have made a great husband and father for some lady and he is a good dancer for a priest.'

As Father Millinus and I danced, the king and queen joined the fray and danced beside us and so Catherine and Trist joined the group, then came Elia and a young man and Miranda grabbed up Buddy and proceeded to use him as a dance partner. Of course Buddy didn't mind as long as someone gave him attention. He was one happy, loving dog. Myra, Vilian joined in holding hands and dancing and Nathisa jumped on the floor grabbing a guard and asking him to protect her from dancing alone. Soon it seemed as if the whole court joined into the dance. The music began to die down and the lights began to burn low and slowly people began to slink out of the festival and carefully make their way back to their homes. The festival had run for quite awhile from 6:00 pm. to 4:00 am. in the morning for the most hardy partiers. But alas, as with all good things, this too had to come to an end.

The king and his court began to filter back to the castle and finally the music came to a complete stop and the lights burnt down completely. All just before sunrise, some of the servants that had left the festival early on in the night had risen up and began to take the decorations and torches down and gather up all of the remaining food and leftovers which were to be given to the Order of Palin that they might feed the homeless and orphans in the kingdom. The other girls and I were being escorted to our rooms by guards and one by one we entered into our rooms and undressed and lay down for a few hours of sleep.

I entered into my room and found Buddy just sitting there upon my bed looking up at me as if to say, 'What kept you? I've been alone for hours in this room. Where were you all night?'

"Oh, Buddy! Don't look at me like that! I'm very tired and I have to get some sleep. Get off my bed or at least move over after I get out of this gown. I'm going to be jumping into my bed and into my covers so you better be out of the way or it might be a bad end to a day for the both of us."

Suddenly a knock came from her door. I answered, "I can't answer the door. I'm not decent." A quiet female voice whispered, "It's me. You can open the door. I'm all alone. No one will see." I walked quietly over to the door and opened it up ever so slightly and Nathisa pushed her way in and shut the door abruptly.

"Oh Sahnedra, thank you for introducing me to your friends and for letting me stay around you most of the night. I really appreciate it. It meant a lot to me and in a little while, I will pay you back for your kindness in ways you can't imagine. I will make your life like a million lives! Will you accept my gift?"

I replied, "There's no need for that. I just want to be your friend and all but if you want to give me something or would like to trade, I'm ok with that." Nathisa grabbed me by the waist and pulled me close to her and proceeded to kiss me on the mouth and said, "You and I will be friends for life, however long that may be whether it is one day or a million. You are my eternal sister and I will love you as such. Good night and thank you for the wonderful evening. Please don't allow anyone to disturb my sleep. I'm so tired. See you tonight sister." And with that, Nathisa walked to the door and proceeded to leave.

I was quite taken aback by what had just taken place, but continued to undress and get ready for bed. And I thought to myself, "Another sister. Oh, great! Just what I needed, but I like her. Maybe this one will be worth having."

As I slept, I couldn't help continually waking up every few hours with horrific daymares. In one, I saw darkness enclosing around me and speaking to me almost calling out my name, 'Sahnedra, Sahnedra, Sahnedra! Come to me! Join me! Listen to the sounds of my voice! We must have you! We'll protect you from death, disease and harm. We will have you or you will **die**!'

I jumped up and screamed a scream that could be heard down the corridors of the whole castle, "I don't want to die!!"

CHAPTER 7

The attacks begin.

After my screaming had awakened everyone up in the entire castle, my hand was laid hold upon by Mercia. "Sahnedra, what's the matter? What has given you such a bad morning's sleep? Did you eat something that didn't agree with you?" While she was asking me these questions, I apparently stared at her in a gaze not knowing what to say or how to answer her.

All the guards were at alert and many were patrolling the grounds and outer walls of the castle and yet others were sent by Justarly to scout out the town and the countryside to make sure nothing was around that might be trying to put a spell on the royals and the quest of the kingdom. All the men were armed and had heavy suits of armor on with the orders to stop anyone that doesn't belong on the grounds or in the castle without express orders from the king or his queen or family. Father Millinus came in suddenly and began to pray a prayer over me and my room and yet other priests from his order were lighting candles and burning incense to try and rid the room of any perhaps evil spirits that might have entered the castle from the night's previous festivities, but still my visions remained and I could still hear small but faint voices in my head that were calling out for me.

Voices that wanted to speak to me about something but yet they wouldn't say who or where they were or what they wanted. What could all this mean? I didn't know then, but I fully understand now. What they wanted was me and all I could bring to them in the form of power, beauty and influence. That is what the world thrives on after all, isn't it?

After all the ins and outs were done, I was assured by everyone in my house and family that I would be fine and it was just a dream. Maybe my mind was running away with me after having tasted some of the finer things that our kingdom had to offer at last night's festival. Maybe it was just too many sips of wine a sip of wine. What else could it be? Well, I don't care what anyone says. It seemed real to me and I just hoped they were right and that it was a dream.

I proceeded to go and wipe my eyes and began to fix my hair with the aid of a few girls that help me with such things. I chose a dress to wear and a pair of boots so I could go out and do some day riding with Nathisa if she felt up to it after all we had been through over the last evening.

I got up and out of my room and left the night behind and went to Nathisa's room and said, "Nathisa, are you up?" Behind the door I could hear her reply, "No, not yet, Sahnedra. Come get me later this evening. I'm really tired because of my long journey and the ball we attended last night. And oh, I hope you are all right. I heard you scream something awful." I replied, "Oh, thank you, Nathisa. I'm fine. I think it was only a bad dream and I had something rest on my stomach that may have soured and maybe it had given me an awful dream. But it seemed so real to me, very vivid."

Nathisa responded, "I wouldn't worry about it. I get those dreams all the time. In time you can learn to control your dreams if you try hard enough, but if you don't mind, I will join you at supper time this evening after I rest up and maybe we can ride later tonight or early tomorrow morning if you would like." I answered, "Okay, I will see you later. Have a good rest and hopefully you will feel up to riding later this afternoon."

So, I proceeded to go out to the courtyard and ran about to find my horse and sure enough Buddy was following my every step. I tried to lose him because I didn't want him giving away my intentions of going for a small ride around the countryside. As I entered the stables, there was Drang and Clive making sure that the horses were all cleaned and fed and instructing the men with them on how to organize their armor and coloring for the army standards.

Clive asked, "Sahnedra, what are you doing here? I mean, it is always wonderful to see you, my princess, but right now we are really busy and we need to get these chores done so we can move on and do the rest of our labors today. Is there anything that I can do to help you?" I replied, "I want my horse Nightmare. Bring her to me. I haven't given her a good working out for months and I'm bored and tired of being a plant and being stuck inside in this hideous castle." Drang warned, "Sahnedra, you know about the dangers that are in the kingdom at this time. Don't you care about what this would do to your mother and father if something happened to you? "I won't try and stop you if you really want to go because I frankly don't have the time for such petty things right now, but I do expect that you have cleared this already with your Father before you go, haven't you?"

I stated, "Of course! You don't think I'm that stupid that I would just go and do something without telling my parents, do you?" So, give me my horse." Drang began to move over to the right and gently pulled on the horse's rein leading Nightmare toward Sahnedra. "Oh, there's a beautiful good girl! Such a lovely animal. So sweet, kind and faithful. Come on Nightmare. Let's go and run a few paths through the countryside while its daylight and safe for travel so these two young men don't faint that a poor helpless little girl such as myself would get hurt by some big, bad beast or something. Bye, guys! See you in an hour or so." And with a wave, I was up on my horse and tearing a trail out of the courtyard and into the town. I was free. At last, I could slow down and just trot at a slow but pleasant pace and take in all the hills, grasses and trees that were all around me. I steered Nightmare towards one of my favorite trails and we proceeded to venture out onto the path and followed it to a very small creek. I slid off my horse and moseyed down to the creek and placed my hand into it for a drink of water and then grabbed Nightmare and led her to the water so she could take a drink and rest a while as well. I pulled a small piece of bread from my bag and began to eat it all the while I pulled some small grasses and the like and gently placed them up to Nightmare's mouth that she could eat as well.

I bent down to get another taste of water when I saw standing above me a man in an old worn out pair of boots. "What is such a pretty one doing here in these parts all alone especially with all that is going on nowadays?" I stood up in a gasp and said, "Who are you and what do you want?"

"I want nothing but your horse and your money and any food you might have and if you don't have it, then maybe we can see that you go fetch me some or things might get bad for you."

I bluntly responded, "I asked for your name and for your info. I only had the one piece of bread and I currently have no money and there is absolutely no way you are getting my horse." The man retorted, "We will see about that." He proceeded to leap off the rock ledge overlooking me on the other side of the creek bank. I grabbed my horse and proceeded to try and jump on Nightmare and as I began to turn the horse to run, the man grabbed me by the leg and threw me off of the horse and to the ground. I hit hard and landed upon the rocks in the midst of the shallow creek. All the while struggling to get up and try and defend myself, all I could see was a haze and I felt as if I was spinning around. The man lunged at me and grabbed me and shoved me to the ground while I continued to kick and thrash and scream. Then Nightmare stomped and reared up and proceeded to run off leaving me in the grasp of this big man that just looked at me and said, "I'm going to teach you a very hard lesson now, little one." He pushed my head under the water and proceeded to drag me to the shore line. While he was pulling me to the shore, I fell down a few times still trying to scream for help and tried with all my might to fight off my assailant. He pulled me up to his face and squeezed my wrist and said, "Now we will see how much fight you have and how much talk you will have when you know your true place in the forest, missy." He shoved me down to the ground while grabbing the base of my neck and proceeded to hold me down with just one arm. I violently kicked and pushed but he had me with such immense force and strength that I could hardly lift up my arms without him pressing them back down with his other arm.

While the struggle was still happening, I didn't realize that a small group of someone's were watching us both and waiting to decide what to do about the current things that were happening to me. These someone's were hungry and ready to strike. The struggle was increasing and I continued to move and twist and turn. I kicked and pushed and was finally able to land a sharp kick in the man's groin which caused him to wince loudly and fall backwards. I quickly began to climb up the small hill leading to the path. Just at the top of the hill, I could see Nightmare. I began to cry out in a shrill voice, "Nightmare! Come to me! Help me, Nightmare!" Nightmare turned and began to trot towards me and almost sensing I was in danger suddenly began to pick up the pace. The man having recovered got up and proceeded to run at me in a fury and said, "That's it! You're a dead little girl!" I grabbed Nightmare by the reins and pulled myself up on my horse and the man proceeded to grab me by the leg and was pulling with all his might to pull me off, but this time Nightmare turned her body all the way around and rose up and knocked the big man down. I had a death grip on Nightmare and wrapped her arms around her neck and held onto her mane and kicked her and Nightmare proceeded to follow the path down back to the field that led to the edge of the forest path.

While Nightmare had taken off and rushed back to the edge of the forest path, a sudden blood curdling scream could be heard in the distant background almost as if it had come from the place that I, Nightmare and the man had just come from. "Help! Help me! No! No! Stop! Ugh! Ouch! No! Aw!"

I didn't know if I had truly heard this or if I was fading in and out of consciousness. All I knew was that I had to stay on Nightmare and hope that Nightmare would find her way home like she had done so many times before in the past.

As the day began to pass, several patrols were sent out to make sure that the surrounding countryside was safe and secure and one of them happened upon me. They found me bruised and beaten. I had a black eye and cuts on my forehead and bruises upon my legs, but other than that, I appeared all right. The patrolling guards grabbed my horse and wrapped a blanket around me and led me and Nightmare back to the castle. There, I was promptly given to Father Millinus for care and supervision.

"Sahnedra, Sahnedra, are you awake? You gave us quite a scare! Can you tell me what happened?" I weakly responded, "Yes, Father, I was attacked." Father Millinus acknowledged, "Yes, child, we all can see that and your Father has sent out patrols all over the countryside seeking whoever attacked you but can you tell me and your Mother where it took place and who it was that attacked you?" I replied, "I would have to take you there. It was my special place over the hill meadows and on a secret path I made years ago through the forest to a small creek bed where I like to sit and think and eat and look at all the wonders of nature." Vinician spoke up, "Just tell your Father's men how to get there and then they will find it. There is no reason for you to go and see the place of such an attack again." "No, Mother, I want to show them where it is because I thought..." Vinician queried, "You thought what, Sahnedra? No, don't play games with me because I have half a mind to beat you when you get better just for doing something so stupid! We've been told that you told Drang that you had our permission to go and trot about all over the countryside and for him and Clive not to try and stop you. Is that true, young lady?" I could see that this was going to be a long evening and that I needed to appease my Mother fast if I was going to keep what was left of my body intact.

Peeking around the corner of the room, Nathisa appeared and said, "Excuse me, but can I come in?" Vinician said, "Of course, come on in and see what stupidity can cause to happen if one doesn't keep everyone informed as to one's true intentions, right Sahnedra?" I just smirked as Nathisa inched closer to me and grabbed me by the hand and began to speak. "Sahnedra, if you want, I will ride out with you and your Father's men tomorrow morning to help you locate the place you say you were attacked." I answered, "Yes, please help me convince my Mother of what I'm saying is the right thing to do because I need to see what happened. I thought that I heard the man screaming in pain as though he was attacked right after I escaped on Nightmare."

Father Millinus chimed in and said, "My queen, you know it is quite possible that Sahnedra going to the place might help her and it could help us see if we can find where some of the thieves are that are trying to take advantage of this recent blight that has come upon our beloved kingdom." Queen Vinician consented, "Alright, Father, if you think that it is best, I will consent to what you believe at this time. Please do this first thing in the morning and bring her back safe and see to her wounds and try to cover them if possible." Father Millinus bowed and said, "Yes, my queen."

With the word of Father Millinus, Queen Vinician walked out of the room followed by her guards and court advisors. Father Millinus looked at me and Nathisa and winked and said, "Can't you both see that when we do this tomorrow we will all need to stay very attentive as to our surroundings and try and find any clues we can as to what happened? But right now, Sahnedra, you need to get some rest and recover all of your strength because we have a small, but important journey for tomorrow."

Nathisa said, "I will stay with her for a while, Father." Father Millinus looked and smiled and then proceeded to bow and slowly turn and exited the room. When Father Millinus had left the room, Nathisa then got up and silently but gently shut the door and turned and looked at me and stated, "There is much to be done and much to be said about the goings on in this kingdom. Many years ago in Russia, we had some of the same odd occurrences take place until we killed off what was attacking us. I don't know all the story, but I will tell you what I can at a later time and day, but I cannot at this time because you will want to rest and I will need my strength as well to ride out in the day's sun." I asked, "Why do you not like the sun? It is so bright, warm and beautiful?" Nathisa smiled, "Some in the Russian royal line have a disease that afflicts us and that disease is that when we go out in direct sun our skin burns and we get sick because of it. I have this disease, but have begun in the last several years to begin to tolerate this and am thinking that I might be getting healed of it because I can now go out as long as I'm covered and not standing in the direct sunlight for too long. I'm now more able to bear the heat of the sun on my body."

Nathisa then said, "Let me look at that cut on your head, it looks like it hurts." "It does," I replied. Then Nathisa reached out her hand and wiped my forehead and took it to her lips and licked her fingers and rubbed my head again and again the fingers went to her lips and see closed her eyes and said, "Oh, such strength you must have to have withstood such an assault. May that evil man be found and torn apart!" I asked, "Did you just lick my head with your hand and drink my blood?" Nathisa replied, "No, my dear, I did not. I simply licked my hands and posted it to your forehead to cool you down and to wipe your head clean of any dried blood. Just like one would do a dear loved one if they were hurt. Perhaps you are too tired and your eyes are playing tricks on you after such a violent occurrence." With that, Nathisa grabbed my neck and looked me straight in the eye and said, "We will find this dog and punish him my sister." Then she kissed her lips and said, "Until tomorrow and the hunt, sleep well, and if you need me, don't hesitate to call for me."

After a good night's sleep and no more dreams for the night, I thought it must have been a dream because everything seems so much like a blur the last few days since the festival. Father Millinus, Drang, Stimer, Princess Nathisa and a couple of priests from the Order of Palin mounted their horses and proceeded to follow the same path that I had taken the proceeding day. The king's patrols had only covered part of the ground where they had found me but had failed to find the path from which I had taken to get to my private hiding spot away from the world. And it was no surprise to me that the patrols couldn't find it because I had made sure it would be hard to find by taking and weaving in and out of this area and that going from this small mound to this large, grassy field to the minor creek and then turning up a small hole to where you find a small gap between two large trees that then clearly showed a barely worn path made by horse hooves. This small path led over a few small hills and took one up a couple or larger hills down a deep valley and to a small ledge that one could easily go down to a small rocky outcropping to the creek below. Eventually, I would have to find another faraway place yet close enough to the castle to hide by myself that is if my mother would ever let me out of her sight again.

Upon finding the place of the attack, the entire group and I all proceeded to leap down from their rides and what they saw was horrifying. Bits and pieces of clothing were lying all over the ground from a full grown man that apparently had them shredded off his body while he was still wearing them and fighting off a would-be attacker or group of attackers.

Father Millinus asked, "Sahnedra, you didn't do all this?"

"No Father, I barely hurt the man at all. You can see where my body made an indent on the ground in the creek where he threw me from my horse when I first tried to escape and then look at how the rocks and dirt are messed up where he proceeded to attack me." Nathisa exclaimed, "Well, something tore this evil man up and look!" Nathisa screamed so loud that it would seem the whole forest came to life. "A leg bone and over there is another piece of skin and look in the tree branch! A half devoured arm!" Father Millinus stepped up with his brothers from the Order and began to bag up a few clues to take back to the castle so he could show them to the king and for Drang to view and study to try and find out what had happened in this neck of the woods. Drang ordered, "Clive, get a bag so we can bury whatever remains the Father doesn't want or need." I was walking around the small bend in the creek when I turned and jumped back and fell into the water. There before me was the half-eaten skull of the man who had attacked me and his back plates and bones were almost standing stuck in a branch that almost reached down to the creek itself. The men grabbed Nathisa and I and placed us up by the horses and we began to whisper amongst ourselves. One of the younger priests went a little further down the creek and proceeded to throw up violently. Father Millinus went to him and rubbed his back and spoke to him about how it takes a while for a man's stomach to deal with the stink of death and the effects of seeing another human being dismembered and that in no way reflects his lack of being a man or servant of the Most High God, but rather shows the great mercy of God in that he feels sympathy for the harm of one of God's higher creatures. As Clive was looking around the scene of the attacks, he pointed out to Drang the various forms of footprints. Some were men, some appeared to morph into a beast print like a very large wolf and yet there were clear signs of my tracks before and during the attack and where I had crawled up to my horse because you could clearly see drag marks on the ground.

And Drang pointed out to Father Millinus who proceeded to cut out and around some of the footprints claw markings on the ground and yes, one could see where the man that had attacked me was standing and walking. Knee marks were on the ground from where he attempted to attack me in the muddy bank. But when the man was apparently attacked, there were no further footprints. But deeper and deeper footprints are found of a man that must have formed into a beast. "It is almost as if the man was lifted up above the head of the creature that attacked him and carried around until he was dismembered," said Father Millinus.

Drang queried, "Is such a thing possible? I've lived in this area all my life and besides a few cats, wolves and bears, nothing can or would dare attack a grown man let alone lift him above its head or body. I mean they may drag you around if they are big enough, but not lift you above their head. Not even a horse lifts you up. One must mount a horse and then lead the horse where one wants to go. But it won't lift you up by its own power above its head. That just isn't the order of nature."

Clive chimed in, "What if we aren't dealing with nature at all? Could this be some form of demon that has crossed over to our world?"

Father Millinus responded, "Now boys, don't get carried away as yet. We have young, inexperienced priests with us and don't forget the princesses that are here. We must first get the items we have come to get and take them back and discuss our findings with the royal house and all the advisors. And remember, if it is in our realm, then I believe no matter how hard or large we can make it bleed and if it bleeds, then we can by God's might make it die."

The small band proceeded to go from the creek bank up the small trail and back towards the castle. The day had wasted away very quickly seeing as the small band kept finding more and more markings on the route of the path back. And they couldn't help but notice that several trees had deep claw marks in them almost like marking posts that was marking new and undiscovered country or was it a marking that pointed the way to its next victims?

While riding, Clive spoke and said, "I don't know about you guys, but I can't wait to get back to the barracks so I can bathe and get some warm food in my belly." Drang replied, "Yeah, leave it to you to see all the mess and yuck of today and all you can think about is your stomach. It's amazing you don't weigh a ton with as much food as you put away my friend. Ha! Ha! Ha!" All those present laughed and chided each other along the way back to the castle and when they had finally reached the meadow that lead back to town. I began to shout, "Look at the castle! It's on fire! My home is on fire!"

CHAPTER 8

The heat of fire turns into a cold night.

As our party hurried to race to Satu Mare castle, I could plainly see that the fire was in the process of consuming it. Big billows of black smoke were ascending out of various windows and the wind just seemed to add to the chaos that was going on by intensifying the rage of the flames. We finally reached the edge of town and the fire was by now seemingly intensifying itself and it seemed to be enraged as if it had a mind and will of its own. The flames seemed to have wanted to destroy and consume anything or anyone that was getting in its way and trying to prevent it from devouring its intended victims which in this case was my home.

As we hurriedly traveled up the rocky path to the edge of the town, we watched as the whole area was abuzz with movement and scenes of horror and chaos. People were loading up wagons and buggies as fast as they could. Some were fetching pails and buckets to bring them to the men at the castle who were trying to fight the fire. Others were busy throwing water on their own houses to try and save them in case the fire was to spread out past the walls of the castle. The scene was utter chaos and horror as we continued to travel down to the outer court and then rushing into the inner court. There we were met by armed guards and Trist and he told us to hold place and not more any further because the men past this point were busy rushing about fetching water sand and dirt to throw upon the flames which by now had engulfed what appeared to be the entire castle.

As the castle burned, I wondered what would happen if it was gone by the end of the day or by early that evening. I held onto Nightmare and was really in a state of shock not knowing if everyone in my family was okay. Was Buddy all right? Did he get out? What about all of the servants and my girlfriends? Did they all make it out unharmed? Are they all right and alive? What if someone dies from this awful fire? Where will I live? All that and a million other questions raced my mind. Nathisa seemingly sensing my fear and confusion pulled up beside me and reached over and patted my hand and said, "It will be okay, all will be fine."

Suddenly I saw Father Millinus leap off of his horse and the priest with him followed as he began to tend to several men that had come out of the inner court of the castle. It appeared as though they had been burnt and had skin that was blackened and a few seemed to have skin hanging from their face and neck areas of their bodies. Father Millinus and the brothers that were with him grabbed various ointments and wraps that they always carried with them wherever they went and began to apply them to the wounds of the victims of the fire.

Father Millinus began to pray and wrap up a man all at the same time asking him questions as he was trying to figure out what had happened and what could have caused such an angry fire that engulfed the castle in such a short time. One of the men that was wounded was a priest of the Order of High Palin and as one of the priests were tending his wounds said, "Ralisu set the fire and ran throughout the courtyard and tossed a lit torch in the horse stables and then he had went into the kitchen and lit fires there as well." Father Millinus asked, "Why would he do such a thing?" The wounded priest replied, "Because he was tired of being held like a prisoner in a castle that he was trying to defend and then he tossed some of us around and ran off like a wild man." Father Millinus then inquired, "So did you see him light the fires?" The wounded priest answered, "No, I didn't exactly see him, but after he broke free from us that is when the fires were seen to be breaking out all over the place." Father Millinus replied, "Brother, if you didn't see a man do something for yourself then you can't accuse him of doing it. Otherwise it is just a coincidence and nothing more. He may have done it but if you didn't see it, then you may be condemning a man unfairly that may be innocent of the charges you are placing against him."

With that, Father Millinus proceeded to finish caring for the men around him and Trist and the others were busy watching for any signs of anyone trying to set more fires around the area. As time went on, the fire got hotter and the light of the sky was filled with the smell of burnt wood, charred mud, bodies and death. Smoke was everywhere and it began to blow our way due to the increase in the winds. As the day continued to pass and at the night's midway point, the castle was no more. At least not in the sense that it was when it filled the skyline of Satu Mare with its full glory.

My castle, my home was gone at least for now as night continued upon us and it waxed later and later into the evening. I could finally make out the figure of a man all dirty and he seemed to be covered in soot. It was Father and then I saw Buddy running right by his side coming to us and after him, I saw my sisters, friends and other important members of the court and the various house servants. My heart was relieved and jumping for joy! One by one they came out and we began to form a circle as if everyone was gathering around to hear what Father was about to say and to see if he had any great words of encouragement or wisdom for such a time as this. Justarly was proceeding ever so slowly with his group and a small band of the queen's guards were following him. All of them seemed to be burned very badly so several members of the Order of Palin had rushed to their sides and proceeded to wash their wounds and pour various oils on their burns and then they began to wrap the wounds in a way to try and fight infection to keep it from taking hold in any open wounds.

Father spoke up, "Justarly, where is queen Vinician?" Justarly responded, "Sir, I don't know, I haven't seen her since we had been fighting the fire that broke out in the queen's corner of the castle. The last I knew is that I had a few men try and escort her out of harm's way as I and the four men with me tried to hold the fire back and put it out. We truly made every effort to stop the fire in its tracks but we could not." Father asked, "Has anyone seen any of these men or the queen?" No one replied in the affirmative but then all was silent.

Father Millinus spoke up and said, "Let us begin a search for them now." Trist responded, "No one can enter the area around the castle for at least the remainder of the night and maybe until tomorrow evening. We are still putting out small fires in areas of the castle that keep flaring up and portions of the castle may be unsafe to enter right now due to structural weaknesses that the fire has caused. So before anyone enters anywhere, I must be sure as the king's head guard that the castle is safe and secure for any and all who might desire to venture into it to salvage whatever remains and that includes any survivors or human remains." Father spoke up, "Trist, it's my wife and I want to be sure she is safe and unharmed and I mean NOW!"

Trist immediately responded, "Sorry, sir, it's not going to happen or I will resign my commission right now. I swore an oath to protect and serve you and this people and if I allow anyone including you my king to enter a place that has been attacked by anything before I know it is safe and secure, then I am failing in my duty and I didn't take this position to fail but to try and add to the name of Humboldt and all that he had taught me in his many years of service to you. Now, king, if you would not advise against these words if he had said it instead of me, then at least treat me as you would have him. I seek to protect all that could rule and reign over this kingdom just as he had done and I can't protect anyone if they enter a place that might flare back up into a raging fire in a moment's notice because of some strong wind nor can I protect a group that enters into a building that may fall upon their heads at any moment due to a wind or a weakness from some mortar being burnt and weakened. My commission is in your hands dear king but I cannot serve if my words are not hardened too in this matter. Thank you for your time and patience in laying out my case."

Father Millinus stepped forward at that moment between the king and Trist who were very close at the time and interjected, "Dear men, let's step back for a moment and look at this situation as men and not in a rash rage or in haste. King, what Trist says is true. It is his place to try and protect all that fall under his care. He knows that fires are still being fought in various places as they continue to spring up almost out of the ground due to some fat being in this area or a bunch of hay laying around in that place. We all know that the wind is blowing like a demon tonight and is going about blowing embers of fire here, there and everywhere so would it not be wise to allow plenty of time for our men to do their jobs and make sure that we all have complete control over this deadly situation before we venture off into a chase that may not be needed to be in the first place.

I mean per say the queen is on the other side of the town or the men and the queen found their way out the other side of the castle. Maybe she and the men are waiting on us to find them because as you all know we are having the worst problems with repeated flare ups of fire from the east side. That is where the wind is blowing the strongest and where the animals' straw is as well as most of the kitchen fat and meat so the juices of such things will burn with more intense heat. So let's use wisdom and all the men of the kingdom to go out and look for the queen and her party for the next day and night and see if they can be located and thus we can give Trist and his men time to get full control of this whole situation." The king looking enraged backed up and spoke, "Father Millinus and Trist, it is my wife and she is my rib, flesh of my flesh and part of me and I want to be sure she is safe, but I see what you both are saying then. If you my two closest advisors are going to side against me, then at least send some men out from my personal guard and any of the queen's guards as well as any free priests from the Order of Palin and have them scour the city and see if they can find out where the queen is and those men. I don't care if everyone is looking all night long. The queen must be found and I pray to God she's found alive!"

With that Trist and Father Millinus set about sending out men to look for the queen. Trist sent Justarly and his men out. He made sure to have a few men go out with each of the king's lead guards which included Drang, Clive and Stimer. I and Nathisa proceeded to ride about the area seeing if anyone had found or seen the queen and her guard. Trist had Catherine, Elia and Miranda go out with what men they had with them. Groups were sent everywhere to the surrounding areas. Various men and women banded together to join in the search out of concern for the queen and her men. All were busy trying to find the mother of our kingdom and was worried about her fate and her welfare. All because these were dark times in our kingdom and no one knew what to expect next. It seemed like at every turn something new was coming against our little kingdom and sadly it was always seemingly negative or destructive.

So the night waned and the dawn began to break and as yet there was no sign of my Mother and the men that were to escort her to safety. As Father stood on the banks of the small river that border the castle of Satu Mare, he stood then he paced back and forth. One by one small bands came in and gave a report to him about what they had found or what they had seen or even what some had been told by others they stopped to ask questions to but yet there was no sign of my Mother and her party. As early dawn became midday, the stress of not having any news was beginning to show upon Father's face and the others. Most of us had been out all night and no one had slept since the early part of the last day before the fire so fatigue began to be evident upon each of us. And as anyone knows when people get tired, tempers flare and accidents can take place that normally wouldn't happen. It was noted that men fell off of horses exhausted and a woman fell into an open well that had been uncovered during the day of the fire so that the men could have easy access for pulling up water from the ground. A young child slid into a pond during the night while he was trying to do his part in finding the Queen and the list just goes on. Trist, after hearing story after story of accidents taking place after twenty-four hours of non-stop searching called all the leaders of the search parties together and ordered a stop to the searches until everyone had at least six hours of rest. And he ordered the men that were still fighting the few remaining flare ups to take and rotate shifts four hours on and four hours off so they themselves wouldn't be killed or injured while trying to get the castle's fire under complete control.

While Trist was about doing his best to continue looking for the queen, Father Millinus and several of the priests of the Order of Palin were allowed to go back to their area and found everything burnt or destroyed beyond use. The barracks the priests stayed in was gone, the church was severely damaged and the house of Palin where the priests fed the needy and tended to the wound or sickness of the helpless was also badly damaged. Father Palin looked around after having viewed and inspected the scene and said, "Brothers, tear it down. All of it! Tear it down and we will start rebuilding now." So the brothers of Palin began to tear down the barracks first and then they began to tear down the church and then the house of Palin and they did all that within one full day of work. Of course, several of the people of the town also helped them to chop up the wood and then gathered up whatever straw they could find as well as anything that might be used or reused later for building material of the new buildings that the priests and their Order might need.

The people of Satu Mare were a hardy people. They were tough and very willing to work hard when the need arose. They were people who would still do what needs to be done and this is the way the people still are today. As the priests were busy working to tear down and rebuild, Trist and the rest of the court were still fighting the fires that seemed to pop up in one place and then another until the late evening of the second day of the great castle fire.

Father asked, "Trist, when can we begin our search for the queen on the grounds of the castle itself?" Trist replied, "King, it would be best to wait until at least early morning of the next day and here is my reasoning. First of all, that will allow the men that are now rotating in shifts to snuff out any remaining fires with ample water and we can count on the dew to moisten things as well and this will help us to be sure that the area is wet enough that we should have full control over the whole situation." The king questioned, "Okay, I understand and have you heard word from any of our search parties about news of the queen? Has anyone even thought that they seen her?" Justarly replied, "No, my king. We are still out searching but as yet no word has come in. It is thought that the men might have taken the queen to the hidden villa in the forest as a place to retreat to until things calm down. The men may have taken her. They're thinking that I and Trist would take the whole group of royals there as a place of safety and housing until the castle situation is under control and repaired. But that is only a thought that we have just recently come up with because most of us had forgotten about the villa because it is a last ditch place to take the royals in case the castle was overrun by invaders or something horrible had taken place just like this fire." The king replied, "Only Vinician would have thought of that. That sounds so much like her. She always liked the villa because it is just about like our castle, but it is used very little. If she was there, surely she would have contacted us by now and have asked us for provisions and for more guards to insure that she and the villa were safe." Trist replied, "Sir, we aren't saying that she is there but that she may be there and that we may have overlooked the villa because it is a last safe haven the royals are to go to in case of a emergency of some nature. I hardly even remembered it until I and Father Millinus as well as Justarly put our heads together last night while we were having dinner trying to figure out where the queen and her men could be. In fact, if Father Millinus had not suggested it and reminded me that Humboldt had set up the villa as a place of safety for the royals, then we might not have ever thought about it to be honest with you." Father broke in, "Don't worry about that, Trist, those things come with age and experience. I myself as I had stated earlier had all but forgotten about the villa and yes, you both are right Humboldt had me build it for all the royals and maybe visiting ambassadors that might have been in need of special protection during times of kingdomly stress or war and I dare say this event fits that description to a T."

Justarly speaks, "Dear king, you do understand that we don't know if the queen is there, right?" The king peers over at them and stares for a moment and says, "Yes, men, I get it. You don't know for sure. I'm not mad or have lost my mind, but you have given me something now that I didn't have a day ago and that is hope that she might be alive and in a place of our own control. The only other place that she might have fled to would be in the deeper part of the castle basement or even the dungeon by the moat, but I don't know why she wouldn't have came to our group if she was down there unless one or more of the doors or gates are blocked off or they are trapped by falling debris or some other such thing that is likely beyond my imagination at this time."

With that, both men bowed and proceeded about their business. Trist summoned Drang, Clive and Stimer to go with twenty-five men and seek out the villa and see if the queen and her men had made it there and they were also instructed to take two wagons of supplies with them as well to prep the villa for the royals that are in need of a place to stay while the castle and all the adjacent structures are surveyed and torn down and or repaired or replaced.

"Come on men! Let's get a move on! We need to be at the villa by sundown so we can take in what is going on and access the situation," Drang said as he and his small group of thirty men tramped through the streets of the city and the paths of the countryside. He couldn't help but think to himself, 'How did those fires get started and how did they leap from place to place so quickly?

It couldn't have been one man by himself but it had to be many people in many places because we had guards everywhere because of the chaos in the kingdom that has been taking place as of late.'

Stimer exclaimed, "Well, we only have two hours or so more to go before our bums get a break from all this up and down the hills riding. I can't wait to eat and have a nice clean place to lay my head for a night or so." Clive responded, "Don't get used to it. We are going to set it up tonight and maybe during the day tomorrow but if we find the queen, then we are to send word back to the king and then leave the guards at the villa and proceed back to Satu Mare and set about joining the escort for the rest of the royals to come and join whoever is at the villa." Drang interjected, "Well, one of us is going to stay behind because I need one of you to take charge of the villa in my absence until the king arrives there. One of us will have to get busy building up the security of the villa and make it a small fortress until our castle is repaired or rebuilt."

With that, the men all began to talk back and forth about their theories about what had happened and who or what set the fires and other such small talk until finally they arrived at the villa.

As they rode up, a small group of young women were about the villa tending to trees and various small gardens in the area. Some were doing laundry and others were setting up tables for a evening meal. Drang and the group rode up to the area of a garden and a young woman presented her and said, "Hello Sergeant, I hope you are well after your ordeal at the castle the last few days. And I hope that the sisters and I can offer you a fine meal to help refresh you from your long journey today to this place. I am Sister Amanda and these sisters around me are all from the Order of the White so please get off of your horses and allow us to help you unload the wagons and join us for a fine meal. We are preparing for the arrival of the king and the royals as we speak." Drang responded sounding surprised and confused, "How did you know we would be coming? How did you know about the fire? And how did you know to prepare a meal for us?" Sister Amanda answered crisply, "Well, my dear, one question at a time. First of all, we didn't know exactly when you were coming but that you would probably most likely come here to see if the villa was in proper order which as you can see it is. Secondly, we heard of the fire because we have sisters that travel to and fro around the kingdom all the time and we as anyone else catch wind of such important tails and happenings from all over the kingdom and especially such a important matter as to affect the lives of the royals. I mean, you would have to be completely naive to hold such a position as lead Sister of the Whites and not be ready for such a sure thing as the arrival of the royals after a massive fire was said to engulf the whole castle. I mean, really, just because we are in the forest and away from the main of the kingdom don't mean we don't catch word of important events especially one that affects the church and such a great and noble order as the High Order of Palin. Now to how we knew how to prepare for your arrival and this great dinner, well, let me say, we eat at the same time every day and would have eaten if you hadn't arrived anyway and any leftovers would have been wrapped and placed in a dry place for use tomorrow. But I figured from the winds of the words being spread about that a party from the castle would arrive any day now." Drang politely asked, "Well then, before we sit to join you in what looks like a wonderful meal, tell me, is the queen and a small attachment of men here with you?" Sister Amanda responded, "No! We haven't heard or seen the queen. In fact, we figured she was arriving with you and this small party that you have brought to us because it is the custom for the queen to go and make sure everything is in order for the arrival of the king and the rest of the royals."

With that, the small group sat down and began to talk about what had taken place as they ate. Drang was so noticeably concerned about the fate of the queen and the dreaded message that he would have to give to the king on the following day after the journey.

The next morning at the break of light, Drang decided to leave Stimer with the sisters at the villa as well as the twenty-five men of the army. He gathered the young priests that were with him and he and Clive set off to return to Satu Mare and the king to give him the news about what they had found at the villa and the state in which it is currently in.

As Drang and his group reached Satu Mare, he saw the king and many of the court outside doing various duties and the business of the kingdom by the bridge. Drang rode up to the group and dismounted his horse and handed him to one of the men standing by him and proceeded to walk up to Trist and whispered into his ear all that he had heard and seen about the journey that he had undertaken the day before. The king leapt up after noticing that Drang and his men had made it back from the villa and said, "Good man, give me the news! Is my wife and her group at the villa?" Trist replied, "Sir, no, she is not there and the Sisters of White have not seen her nor heard word as to her whereabouts but that doesn't mean she isn't okay."

The king furiously replied, "No? What do you mean, no? That means she is in the castle somewhere and we have to get to her and the men! No more waiting, Trist. As of now, I expect you and your men to do whatever it takes to secure the castle today and get to the basement and then the dungeon if need be so we can find my queen. Do you understand?!"

Father Millinus questioned, "Sir, what if it is not safe?" The king impatiently retorted, "Make it safe! I have waited now these three days and we have still got a couple of fires that keep flaring up in the kitchen, so move on it. My wife is important and I need her. I need her here with me by my side! We have ruled this kingdom now for twenty-two years together and I don't intend to rule it by myself without her. Go find my wife now! They could be hurt or need water or aid of some kind but you must move now and if that isn't clear enough for everyone present, then consider it a royal decree! Get my queen!"

So the men began under Trist's leadership to slowly enter the castle each one with two buckets of water for each hand in case of a flare up of fire in a spot here or there and some of the group brought horses and wagons in with them all loaded with skins of water, wet rags or buckets of water on the wagons or carts. Trist had men fan out in all directions and Father Millinus wanted to help as did others in the royal court but Trist only allowed Father Millinus, himself and Justarly to lead the search for the queen and her guards.

They started out on the ground floor removing debris as they went and finding a burnt body of a person here and there or finding the burnt remains of a small animal or a horse that may have pulled a wagon or cart of water buckets. In a spot or two, a few cattle were found that had ran from the barns that caught fire and their bodies were completely burnt as they apparently were trying to find safety from the fire by fleeing towards what they sensed was water only to be cut off by a huge wall that trapped them in as burning debris fell all around them and upon them. Then the group searched the second, then the third floor, then again they went up to a fifth floor and then to the top of the castle upon the battlements that were high up in the air and only found a few unlucky souls that had not made it out in time. There was nothing which pointed to the queen, so Trist then decided to backtrack to the queen's floor which is a level unto itself on the side of the castle where he and a few men had tried to stop and put out the fire before it overwhelmed them. He followed his steps to where the queen had been escorted to what he believed would have been safety to the king.

As he and the men that were with him followed the apparent movement of a small group of people that he had entrusted to lead the queen to safety, he suddenly notices a burnt metal ring on the wall and how it was partially leaning up as he went around this area in the hallway of the queen's floor. He noticed that the wall opened up and there lie a dead man. It was one of the queen's guards. His body looked fine, but his hand was burnt and blackened. Apparently he had been the one to find the secret passage and grabbed the hot heated handle and opened the wall for the queen and her party to escape into. Past the door, Trist and the men grabbed a few torches as they proceeded down a long, narrow and dark stairway path that proceeded to go down to what seemed like five to six floors or more. Finally, they reached the bottom of the stairs and they proceeded to light a few more torches that were laying around on the floor and they placed them into the torch holder upon the walls around them. As they lit up the room, they found other rooms that were all dark and they proceeded to search them one by one until they found a door at the end of one room that seemed to have a long hallway attached to it.

Well, Trist and Drang proceeded to go down the stairs to what appeared to be the basement area of the castle and again, they lit various torches with those that were with them and began to search every inch of the basement. At this point, Father Millinus suggested that Trist send Clive go back to the king to give him a update as to what they had found and not found thus far. Trist agreed and sent Clive back with a couple of men to help him find his way out of the maze that is the basement and the floors above them.

Trist and Drang finally found the dungeon door which should have led the queen and her men to the outside of the moat area if they were able to find it. Drang cried out, "Queen, are you here? Is anyone here?" No one had answered and so the men went forward further and further down to the moat area. There at the entrance to the moat area they had found two torn bodies of the guards that were with the queen. One was dead by a slash to the throat and another seemed to be almost torn in half as if something had tried to tear him apart. The men marked the spot and continued to go further towards the moat area and as they headed through, they began to see light from the outside but also the flickering light of a few torches. As they traveled up to the area where the light appeared to shine from, they found another body of the queen's guard. This time, the guard had his sword drawn and it was stained in a great amount of blood and this man as well had been killed. It would appear he died from a sudden, swift blow to the back of his head.

And then there it was. To the horror of all involved lay the body of the queen. Her dress was stained in blood and her head was torn off and missing. Her body had a few bite marks on it as though something had tried to eat a part of her, but was interrupted. Perhaps it was the guard that was killed with the drawn sword. Father Millinus slumped down to his knees and began to cry and tried to say a few prayers over the dead men and the queen but he knew how badly this would affect the whole kingdom and worst of all, he knew how this would affect my Father, my sisters and I.

Trist and Drang knew it was impossible to console Father Millinus. They tried to get him to stand to his feet. A couple of priests tried to help him stand up, but Father Millinus had been with my Mother since she was a little child or thereabouts. He considered her the daughter he never had and he grieved for her loss, but not just for himself, but for all those around him, especially my Father. As the band gathered up the bodies of the fallen guards and the queen as well as all the charred human bodies that fell in the castle as well as any animal remains, Trist, Drang and Justarly as well as Father Millinus walked towards my Father with Vinician, my Mother, in his arms. My Father upon seeing what was coming fell down and clutched his heart and began to tear at his clothes. My sisters began to weep uncontrollably and Catherine and the other girls fell down with their faces to the ground and cried with an uncontrollable noise.

The whole court was in tears. Many of the soldiers fell backwards from the shock of the queen being found dead and her guards killed. Many of the city folks upon hearing the news rang the various church bells and a great cry could be heard in the area and then there was myself. I just stood there in unbelief not able to wrap my head around what had just happened or who could have done this awful, cruel thing. When I saw what was happening with Father Millinus carrying the body of my Mother and how it affected my Father, my sisters and others of my friends and family, I fainted and must have fallen in the creek that feeds the moat around our castle, because the next thing I can remember was seeing Nathisa and Clive grabbing me and pulling me soaking wet out of the creek and asking me if I was alright or not. When I awoke from that, I just stood still in Nathisa's arms as she held me and cried. She massaged my head softly and stroked my hair and then kissed my head. After several minutes had passed, she said softly, "Sister, it will be better soon. Hold on. Don't give in to the pain and hatred of an evil person or beast. God will make it alright and your mother is now with Christ in heaven waiting for us all." With that, I grabbed onto her and pushed my face into her chest as far as I could try to feel the warmth of a mother's touch at least for one more time.

I can't believe that a such a heat from a fire could turn into such a cold night.

The next day, Father Millinus had fetched Sister Amanda and the Sisters of White from the villa and all were extremely sad and filled with tears and everyone that attended my Mother's funeral procession was wearing the darkest of black. Father Millinus and the High Order of Palin led the procession followed by Justarly and a contingent of the queen's royal guards followed by the black carriage that carried my Mother's casket which was purple with hints of gold on it. The carriage was accompanied by four more royal guards of the king's. Two in the front and two guarding the back and after that was Sister Amanda and the Sisters of White as they followed the black carriage. They threw rose petals to the side and tossed fruit to the crowd and after them was my Father who chose to walk in his royal armor with his royal guards as they followed after the carriage that carried my Mother's body. Trist and Drang kept hold of him to make sure he didn't fall down from all of the stress he had been under while searching for my mother and to keep him appearing strong in the eyes of all of the people because all eyes were upon my Father at this time. Following my dear Father was myself, Myra and Vilian as well as Catherine, Elia and Miranda and following us was the rest of the royals and the royal court were all in procession after that.

We all eventually arrived at my Mother's final resting place where she would lay entombed for the ages until the return of Christ. There my Father sat upon a makeshift throne and was encouraged by his men and all around to sit down because of the weariness which was upon his face. As the body was being lowered, tears began to flow from all who were in attendance and as the casket reached the bottom of the grave, and then Father Millinus began to speak his final prayer over my dear Mother. "Dear Lord, here we are committing this woman back to you. You who gave her to us in the first place. She was not just a queen but also a dear child of the living God. She was like a daughter to me, a sister to me and yes, a dear wise and wonderful friend to me. She was a dear queen to us all but more than that, she was a beloved wife to our dear King Dargon. She was a mother to Sahnedra, Myra and Vilian and as well as a mother to those of our kingdom that had no mother. She in fact was a mother to us all in some way or another and we here today are not weeping for just the loss of a dear queen, friend or sister, but for a mother that is no longer among us. One that will no longer spread her love and joy to us and one that cannot rebuke us when we need it and one that will no longer nurture us with her motherly God given all-abiding love. We today as a people are diminished by this sad loss and we ask dear Father in heaven that you will uphold our troubled kingdom in this hour of need. We have lost a queen, mother, daughter, friend and wife but you, oh God, have gained a pearl. Thank you Father for the time you allowed her to be with us and we ask oh God that you would help us to find the one guilty of such a crime against your people and your kingdom. Help us to mete out stern and swift justice against this crime and strengthen the hands of your anointed, our King Dargon and his dear family and kingdom. Bless us today and receive unto yourself this dear blessed saint into your holy hands, Amen."

And all the crowd present uttered amen afterwards. After the prayer, it began to rain and lightning and the wind became almost violent, so we all hurried into our makeshift houses or tents as we all tried to deal with the events of the past week and what had just transpired. 'What will happen now?' was the last thing I heard my Father say as he approached his tent that afternoon.

CHAPTER 9

The winds of night were blowing.

Now after the funeral of my mother, the queen, it seemed as though the entire kingdom was being blown about like the wind of night. Our castle was gone. The High Order of Palin was busy removing rubbish and rebuilding their buildings as well as their daily other chores and duties such as attending to those in need.

The castle's court was busy being escorted to the villa as well as the various royals, but it was in small groups so as to be sure that the escort could maintain a large enough security guard around them at all times. Along with the servants of the court and the royals, you had various ambassadors and emissaries from various countries that also had to be protected and moved with the royals of our court. And along with their moving, they had to be provided for as well as given a place to stay in the villa which was about half the size of our kingdom's castle.

Another problem our kingdom was facing was gathering up any and all the provisions that were left or remained in usable form from the castle's dungeon, horse stables, etc. All these things had to be moved from the destroyed remains of the castle to the villa until a new castle could be constructed and readied for us all to move back into it.

But that was just the beginning of our issues that we were to face because as of now many of you will remember, that we are now into the middle of spring and we must prepare ourselves to sow the fields and begin to make plans to store the crops when they are harvested. But with the castle gone for the time being and the High Order of Palin crippled at this time that means that our storage capacity is very limited because all we now have for sure at this time to house is the soon to be gathered crops. This will be the granaries of the Order of White and that of the local peoples as well as the various forts that our armies occupy. The big question is, will it be enough to help us make it through the winter season of this year? One will soon find out.

When everyone had finally arrived at the villa, Sister Amanda and the Sisters of the Order of White began by welcoming each group one by one and sat them down for a meal of welcome and then they proceeded to show them to their living quarters for the remainder of their stays. And as you know, there is always someone or some group that will complain about their quarters not being to their likings or that someone else had received more room or space then they did, but Sister Amanda was very apt at getting them to see why they were being placed in the quarters that they had received and why they must abide in that area until the castle could be rebuilt and or repaired.

The villa for the most part was a beautiful picturesque place where you could go and paint a beautiful scene of a countryside. There were four ready dug wells for pulling out fresh mountain water that came down from the melting snow along with a small stream just a few hundred yards away for washing of one's clothing or for use to irrigate the fields that would be sown by the Sisters of the Order of White. And oh, dare I say there were plenty of trees and much green, green grass for horses and cattle to graze upon. The temperature was very pleasant and there was not too much humidity in the air, so for a temporary shelter this place was to me and my friends almost like a small slice of heaven.

But then the winds of the night began to blow again and the dark side of the villa became apparent. During the daytime, everything was pleasant enough and life was pleasing and enjoyable. Father's daily meeting went on with little interruption except for his times when he would tell his court to deal with the affairs of the state in his stead. During these times, Father oftentimes could be seen holding a painting of mother and the family while sitting by the stream in tears. Mostly he tried to keep these times unknown and removed from any other prying eyes, but we all knew that he was having a hard time sleeping as well as keeping his mind upon the affairs of the state.

And it could be seen in the progress of the dealings with the issues that were besetting our kingdom. The kingdom had become under a slow but steady attack over the last several months, and it seemed to increase since the death of mother and the destruction of the castle. Even though Father had instructed Justarly and Trist to keep up the patrols of the surrounding countryside as well as all border regions, well the attacks just continued and what was odd was that it was always against one or two people at a time. No large group of marauders or a small band of Turks or thieves, etc. Just a one or two person group was believed to be going about the countryside killing as they went and for what? No one knew and then there were those people that were being reported to my Father and his court that just simply disappeared. Whole villages had sent out almost everyone into different areas of the country looking for a small boy or girl that had disappeared here or there. Or perhaps a young man was riding on his horse and was sent to the villa to deliver a message to the court and he simply disappeared. No, I'm not talking about just a young man that has never rode a horse before but a young man that is fit and in his prime. One that knows how to ride a horse for many miles and has full control of his beast and knows how to get his beast to go through water as well as over hills and valleys. Young men that would in a few years be apt and ready for the service of our kingdom and ready to join the ranks of our small but powerful army.

For young men like this, villages were also out looking and scouring the countryside for and yet no one ever found a body or any signs of trouble. No clothing was ever found and the horses also seemed to just simply vanish into thin air and no one from the local farmer to any of our generals had the slightest idea what was going on or what was happening in our kingdom.

But the winds of night blew badly during the daytime but it was the nighttime that began to shake even the nerves of our sturdiest soldiers because at night the atmosphere changed from a warm, pleasant place to one of outright fear and dread. The air went from warm to downright cold and the dew seemed to freeze on everything that it found itself resting upon until early the next morning. The sounds of birds whistling in the morning or during the day were replaced by the howling of groups of wolves and coyotes. Sounds of large cats could be heard in the dark as well as a growl of a bear here and there. Various shrieks and screams could be heard in the distance as well as the ever present feeling of being watched by unseen eyes. Trist said that we were being silly and that it was just because we were in a new and different place. He also mentioned that it might take us all a little time to get used to the new arrangements that we found ourselves in and that in time we would grow accustomed to the new environment and its various noises. But I never quite believed that he himself wasn't just a little taken aback by how suddenly things changed after the sunset over the villa. It was just too different and too unworldly, almost like going from this life to the next. Yes, that is what it is. It's like going from life to something seeking to bring you to death's door.

"Sahnedra!" Dargon cried out, "Where are you?" "Over here, Father. What do you need?" Sahnedra yelled back. "Finish getting in order and grab Nathisa and your other friends and prepare to join me at the front of the villa. I have a few guests that are coming and you need to stand in for your mother. And your friends need to take the young ladies that are coming with this group of emissaries and show them around the rest of the villa and keep them busy while you and I sort out this trade agreement with a neighboring kingdom."

"Yes, Father, but what do we need Nathisa for?" Dargon responded, "She will stand on your left during the trade negotiations and help and perhaps see if they would like to do some trading with the kingdom of Moscow and perhaps if everything goes right, then her father's kingdom will increase trade with us and thus it will benefit both our peoples. We get what we need and they get more of what they need. Everybody wins." Dargon said with a grin on his face.

So, I knocked on my friend's doors and said, "Come on, girls. It's time to put on another show of our lives and make sure you look good because how we appear speaks to the glory and honor of our kingdom." Catherine, Elia and Miranda leapt out of their rooms and grabbed their skirts and started to rush after me. "Nathisa," I said while knocking on the door. "Are you ready to stand with us at the trade negotiations?" "Yes, I'm ready little sister. Do you know who it is that we are going to deal with today?" Nathisa asked. "No, not yet. Father didn't say, but I think they are near the Hungarian enclave of kingdoms so they must have lots to trade." "Okay, I'm ready now." Nathisa spoke while slowly opening the door. "Okay, so let's go and make some deals for the both of our kingdoms," Nathisa said with a winch as she finished pulling on her slipper and hopped along the hall as she went.

At the end of the hallway, we were met by Father and Father Millinus as well as Trist who had a royal guard present and Drang had set up the red carpet in preparation to receiving our guests from the visiting kingdom. We met the emissaries and Father introduced each of us to them and then we proceeded to the great hall in the villa which to me wasn't so great and in fact it was quite small considering how large the great hall of our castle was, but as we all knew it was what it was and we were currently stuck in the villa and not the glorious castle to which we all were accustomed to.

Father asked Durant who was the chief emissary of the kingdom of Hungary and the surrounding areas and if he would like to sit down at the table and drink of water, wine or anything else that he desired. Father was also quick to apologize for the small accommodations due to our kingdom's loss of its castle at this time.

"No worries or need to apologize for any of the troubles that have befallen you and your kingdom as of late, King Dargon. These are troubling times for us all and that is why I and my small band have been sent to all the surrounding kingdoms in seek of trade and accommodation for the kingdoms which I represent. I have been give full dispensation to speak for the three kingdoms that make up the great kingdom of Hungary, so all trade negotiations that I make with you will be in force from the moment we sign a treaty of trade." "Excellent," Father responded with a large grin on his face. "And with that, I have something that I think may please you and your kingdom just a little bit more. To show you and the three kingdoms that we of the kingdom of Satu Mare are not just good and honest trading partners, but also a powerful host to great nations beyond our local borders, I would like for you to consider also making a trade agreement with the kingdom of Moscow or Russia. I have already introduced you to Nathisa and she as well has all the power and authority of her kingdom to ink or pen a treaty with anyone that might desire to trade with them as well as us. I'm sure you can see what kind of benefit that this would have for the kingdoms of which you now represent."

With that, Nathisa said, "Yes, Durant, should you desire a treaty then be fully aware that my voice is as the voice of my father's and my signature is set up now to be as binding in any treaty as his would be."

Tilting his head down, Durant acknowledged her trading offer. "That would be most helpful and not to say the least a surprising coo for me to bring back not just a long sought after trading agreement with Satu Mare, but also the kingdom of Moscow, Russia as well. I would be looked at as the greatest trade maker of all times in the history of the kingdoms of Hungary. Yes, I do indeed think I'm interested in pursuing a trade agreement with both of your kingdoms, so shall we proceed?"

And with that, I was forced to sit and watch and listen to hours of talk about everything from the important items that would be traded to the worthless nonsense that filled the room. All the chatter that was going on back and forth for hours seemed to me like a form of living death until finally a full agreement with both countries was formally written out and agreed upon by all three parties. All I did was sit and wonder why me. I hated it. All eight hours of it. Why did I have to waste my day sitting by my Father? I didn't do anything and hardly said a word except for yes or no thank you.

Mother would have spoken and been a direct part of the negotiations. Nathisa's father made her a co-equal with the ability to sign any treaty and it would be enforced as though He himself had signed it! Oh, I'm so tired of just listening and not really doing anything but being seen.

Oh, how I wish Mother was still here. I know that sounds so selfish but I don't mean it to be so. I really wish she was here because I'm useless in these trade negotiations and I'm tired of being Mother's fill-in. Minus the power and authority, if I'm a part, then I would like to be a full part and not just a pretty face in a crown just waiting for the next old man to eye me up and down wondering what it would take for me to be added into the trade for his son.

As Nathisa and I were leaving the room, I said, "Nathisa?" "Yes?" she replied warmly with a large grin on her face. "How did you gain your families trust so completely that your Father has given you his power and authority to trade and make agreements in his stead?" I asked with a solemn face. "Well, little sister, what you need to understand is that I had to sit still and listen. I never got what I have now without playing the game of thrones. It is a long and boring game to us both but it is a game that has been set up by the powers that be and it is in a sense a language. When you understand its language and you learn how to speak it, then you will see that you don't have to ask for the power or authority but that people give it to you freely. I could see that you were so bored you would have loved to have thrown knives at Durant and his company the whole night long. Am I right?"

"Yes," I responded. "Did you see the way he looked at us? He eyed us like we were an entree just waiting to be consumed at the next course of the dinner. It bugged me that Father was so drunk that he never even cared or noticed to say anything to this stranger. He just went on talking about the trade agreement and I'm not for trade and I dont want to be traded off for some dirty old royal's son. I'm a person and I want to choose who I want to marry." I sounded off in a roar as they walked down a small curve corridor.

"Well, little sister, that is part of the problem. Your Mother and mine are supposed to look good for the glory of the kingdoms they represent as you and I will one day. But they also knew the language of power and they used it to make themselves as powerful as the ones that welded the power of the throne. You and I may not get to choose our life mates. Did your Mother choose your Father?" Nathisa asked while peering down the corridor. I responded, "No, my Mother never planned on marrying my Father. She was betrothed to him by her parents in an effort to stabilize regional peace." Nathisa commented, "And the same will be true with you, Sahnedra. You will gain power soon and I can see it in your Father's eyes as well as all the eyes of those in the court from your friends, sisters and everyone else. Since your Mother's death, their eyes are now all turning to you. Did you notice how Father Millinus asked you about the quality of the milk your kingdom agreed to trade with the kingdom of Hungary?" Nathisa asked in passing.

"No, I didn't. I just figured he wondered what I thought of the taste. Why?" I said with a look of bewilderment. "Well, he asked you if you thought it tasted good for a reason. He asked you because he wanted your approval and if you thought it would represent the kingdom of Satu Mare well in trade with the kingdoms of Hungary. My sister, this is just the start of the language of power and you must learn its still nuisances. You have the power of the skirt and you need to realize that when your Father spoke of you today. He didn't speak of you as a child, he spoke of you as a queen in waiting. As if he would leave the kingdom to you should something happen to him. You are not a child any longer, but a woman. A woman that is about to be taught the ultimate language and that is the language of power. If you are willing to learn this language and are willing to let it take you where you need to go to use it, then it will bring itself to you in an ever more present way. Sahnedra, you will never have want of power or authority ever again because you will one day have it either by being on the side of a king or a duke or some such or by simply being a queen of a kingdom. But either way you must learn to hear and understand the language of power." Nathisa said with a hand on my shoulder.

Well, the sun was sitting and the winds of the night began to blow upon all of us that were in the villa. And with it came the usual sounds from the creatures that inhabited the surrounding countryside around us. Frogs sounded to me like battlewagons as they crooked. The night was filled with the fire bugs that glowed and often got just a little too close to the flames of our watch fires and often time feel in due to the intense heat that they emanated. The horses seemed to be restless and the cows seemed to never stop bellowing out. And then of course there was the moving of the tree limbs in the breeze. They looked to me like three men that sought to move ever closer to us but never did. My two sisters seemed to never leave me alone and wanted me to come and talk to them each night until they fell soundly asleep.

Catherine, Elia and Miranda were always busy telling each other stories of the day and what they had seen, heard or experienced. And they always wanted me to come and talk to them so they could find out what was going on in the kingdom and when we would be able to go back to the castle. And then there was Nathisa. I liked her like a sister, but she was always just a little strange to me. She seemed to like to touch me as much as she could and she never needed an excuse to grab me or hug me.

I don't know, maybe I'm being a little strange, but she loved to hold my hand. Maybe it's because she said that she was an only child and never got to go out and make a lot of friends and she very rarely got to play with any other children. So maybe that is why she is always calling me 'little sister.'

'But why does she do what she does?' I thought to myself as I prepared myself for bed. Suddenly, a soft knock on the door could be heard. "Sahnedra, are you in?" Nathisa could be heard asking through the door. I walked over and unlatched the door and replied softly, "Yes, can I help you?" "Oh, yes, please little sister, can I join you in bed? My roof had a leak and my bedroom is all wet along with my bed and I have nowhere else to sleep. Mercia said that she would have the men fix the roof tomorrow after the rain is done and that she would then set about with the other servants to cleaning up and drying out my things, but until then, I have no where or no one else to ask to be with. So please, can I bed down with you tonight?"

"Well, sure. I guess that would be okay because I do have a big bed but I want you to know that I've had some awful dreams as of late and I just can't seem to shake them, so please don't scream if I jump up all of the sudden out of bed or break out into a sweat or something." I replied with a look of fear upon my face.

"No problem, little sister. Maybe me being in bed with you will help you break the circle of bad dreams and the spirits of dreams will leave you alone because they see your big sister is beside you with her arms around you protecting you from them." Nathisa said with a smile as she followed me to bed.

Several hours into the night around one in the morning, I fainted to sleep. All of a sudden, an arm pulled me back against a body; a hard but soft body. From the feel of things, this body was nude and warm but I couldn't see that a hand pulled my head back until I could feel a neck and on my neck I began to feel soft, gentle kisses going up and down my lower earlobe. At my lower ear, I could her a soft voice say, "Sahnedra, my sister, don't fear what is taking place. I have you in my arms and I seek to protect you from all the evil of the world. I have longed for you and a moment like this, please don't reject me, I'm all alone and you are my family so accept me and help me to help you." Nathisa whispered.

I didn't move or speak but held my eyes shut tight. But even so I could feel my heart begin to race and I wasn't sure if it was another dream or nightmare, but whatever the case, it felt real. Sweet, soft kisses were being placed upon my neck and then upon my head.

Now the kisses had moved to my forehead and my lips. Nathisa laid me on my back and began to press her lips with mine. 'No, I can't take anymore! I have to see if I'm awake,' I thought to myself.

Nathisa was laying kisses upon my lower lips. "Nathisa, what are you doing?" I said with a gasp. I started to feel a sense of overwhelming joy while this was taking place. I began to grab Nathisa's thighs and pushed her nether towards my own face and began to lick like I've never licked anything before. I could hear Nathisa moaning and all the while I knew that I was getting her good because I could feel her legs beginning to shake but I just couldn't stop. This was such a release from reality. Then, as suddenly as it started, Nathisa laid down on me and kissed me a time or two more while softly caressing my hair and with that, I suddenly dozed off into a gentle sleep.

Moments later, I felt a sharp pain on my neck. "Ouch!" I felt something grab onto me and I couldn't get it to let go. It was so strong. "Let me go!" And then suddenly darkness had set in on me.

"I'm so tired! What's happening to me?" I said while grabbing my neck.

Nathisa replied, "Don't worry little sister, I'm helping you and I will always protect you forever. It will all be over soon. I love you and you will soon learn the true language of power. This is only a dream and it was a good dream to help you rest from the nightmares that have fermented in your head. Sleep well, little sister. Soon I will raise you up again into the light and you will live forever."

Nathisa covered me up with an old quilt and walked out of the room closing the door behind her. I began to cry out, "I can't move! Am I bleeding? Was it a dream? What's happening to me? Oh, God, help me, it's getting dark! I feel so cold! Please help me! Daddy, Father Millinus, Catherine...anyone?"

CHAPTER 10

From my bed to a casket.

"Sahnedra, Sahnedra, can you hear me my dear?" Father Millinus asked while gently trying to shake me awake. "Did anyone hear anything last night? Anyone? Did any of you hear anything this morning?" Father Millinus again asked while quickly gazing around the room at the group that had gathered.

"No Father, I heard nothing. I just found her like this when I came in to check on her this morning. And the only reason I found her like this was because she didn't answer me when I knocked on the door. This is exactly how I found her. She seems to be okay, but yet she is not answering any questions nor does she respond and look at the sheets and the pillows. There is blood on them like something has bitten her or something. See, look at the lower part of the side of her neck. Have you seen anything like that before?" Mercia spoke with a puzzled look upon her face and her eyes watering with tears.

"No, I've not seen this at all. Not in all my years, but I will have the priests of my order go and research the books of the kingdom of Wisdom and see if they can tell us of anything ever happening since the beginning of time. I will also have a few priests travel to the Order of Old and see if they have ever experienced anything like this in their order's history or books of wisdom."

"This is most worrisome. Most indeed and we cannot allow these weird, hideous things to continue or we could lose the whole kingdom of Satu Mare and worse perhaps the whole world could be swallowed up in eternal darkness." Father Millinus said while summoning the surrounding priests and assigning them their various tasks.

While Father Millinus is taking my temperature and checking my body with the aid of Mercia and Catherine for any other unknown puncture marks or wounds, Dargon rushes into the room with his face in his hands still wearing his nightly robe. "Father, what is going on? Am I losing my mind and does God have it out for me? Have I sinned against Him in some unknowing way? Tell me and I will pay my tithe and tribute to God that He might remove His hand of wrath from me." "No, good King Dargon. This is not the work or wrath of God or His holy avenging angels, but this is the work of a demon or the prince of darkness. It has his handy work all over it. First of all, the beast men and now this blatant attack on our castle is clearly an attack upon our kingdom because you and your army have killed several of these beast men. Do not fear ol' King. God will give us the ultimate triumph, but I may have to ask you for a man or two that can be given by your permission leave from their duties that they might go to Rome for me and light a few more candles for Sahnedra and our kingdom. I would send my own priests but we are now coming to the point of running low on them because of the work of rebuilding the church and the area of good works plus all of the daily chores the brothers perform for the poor of the kingdom. And then yet again, I have sent many of them on various journeys to other areas and ordered them to find out all of the information that I can and of course my King, we are busy doing the works we need to provide for the kingdom, you and the court at the villa." Father Millinus replied.

"You have who and what you need as of now, Father Millinus. Just get it done. Do what you can for my daughter and kill these bastards that are attacking my kingdom and now my family. Trist is in your hands and all of my army that you might need. Just do what you can as fast as you can so we can get back to a normal life. I lost my wife and I can't stand the thought of losing Sahnedra. She is so much like her mother. Please, please heal her and light a thousand candles and if that isn't enough, then light a hundred thousand candles and hire men or women off the street to send up constant prayers for her. Let it be known throughout the kingdom that Princess Sahnedra has been attacked by a force of evil and we need the people to pray for her full recovery." Dargon said while kneeling and shaking in a fit of tears holding my hand to his face.

Father Millinus bowed and beckoned Trist and commanded him to go to Rome and ask for Holy Father Tredo and to tell him all that has befallen the kingdom of Satu Mare and the servants of his church. And he also instructed Trist to make sure to light a thousand candles for me and to have them each blessed with holy oil and prayed over that they might light up the spirit world and get Michael the archangel's attention. So Trist found three of his most trusted men and ordered them to ready themselves to ride with him on a long journey to Rome and to pack provisions for a three month ride there and back or more.

Meanwhile, Catherine was joined by Elia and Miranda and they aided Father Millinus and Mercia in gently moving me while I still seemed to be in a deep sleep from my bed to a cot that was moved beside the bed that Mercia might be able to change the sheets and coverings of the bed and its pillows. Then the ladies began to change my clothing while Father Millinus and all the males of the room had left. After all the changing and cleaning was done, the ladies allowed various members of the court to come in and try to talk to me and coax me awake. But it was all to none effect. I continued to lie in bed motionless and unresponsive from the early morning to the latter part of the day around 7pm. Satu Mare time.

Suddenly, I moved and twitched my hands and then my legs began to shake and as if nothing had been wrong all day, I opened my eyes. The first thing I would see is Myra and Vilian sitting near me holding my hands and gently stroking them as if that might bring the life force back into my cooling body. "Sahnedra's awakened," Myra said with a shout that could be heard throughout the villa. "Sahnedra's still with us, oh thank heavens!" Vilian said while jumping up and hugging my neck. "Oh, ouch, please be careful. My neck and lower back are so sore." I replied while rubbing my neck and grabbing a death grip upon my baby sister whose eyes were streaming with tears. "You all act as if I was dead or something or maybe you've seen a ghost. What is wrong with you?" I said with a look of astonishment upon my face. "Oh, Sahnedra, you've slept all day and no one could awake you. We were so worried that you were dying on us and that you would go to the grave and join Mother in Heaven. Father has been praying for you all day. Trist has been sent to Rome to get Father Tredo and to have a thousand candles blessed by the holy Father and then to have them lit one by one for your safe return to us and your full recovery from whatever it was that had taken and attacked you." Myra said while still stroking my hand. "Please don't leave us! I don't want you to leave us all alone. It would kill Father and who would fight with us? I mean, I know we don't always get along but we don't mean to make you so angry. It's just a joke. Please don't leave us like Mother. We need you." Vilian said with tears messing up her makeup and her red hair waving from one side of her head to the other as she continued to kiss my cheeks and head.

"Don't worry, cherry blossom. I don't plan on dying for a long time. Where's Buddy my dog?" I asked while gently patting Vilian's head. "Buddy was taken by Trist to be blessed by Father Tredo so he could see the spirit beast and protect you from them in the night that they might try to attack you." Vilian said wiping tears away with her sleeve.

Suddenly, the doors burst open and Dargon and Nathisa had rushed into the room. Both of them grabbed me from one side and the other and embraced me so tight that I complained about not being able to breathe.

"Don't you ever do that to me again! Do you want me to die of grief and sorrow?" Father said while stroking my hair and kissing me. "I don't want to ever let you go. You are my firstborn and I can't live without you. You look and remind me so much of your Mother. Please, please stay with us and don't journey into the next world because you might not come back next time." Dargon whimpered. "Oh sister, what happened to you? What caused you to sleep all day and how did you get those wounds on your lower neck?" Nathisa asked with a look of questions upon her face and with her mouth close to my ear. "I love you more than life itself and we are sisters both now and eternally so please don't leave me because you and your family are all I have and you are my best friend in this entire world." Nathisa said while grabbing me in a death grip.

"I won't leave you guys but it is still a little cold and trust me, I think I've got a cold or some such. Could you get me a cover Mercia, please?" I said still shivering and wondering what was going on.

Father Millinus ran into the room holding holy anointing oil from the Order of Palin. "Sahnedra, oh thank God you are here with us still. I've been praying for you since this morning and tried to light candles and bless them all at the same time. I want to anoint you with this holy oil I've brought up and dip you in holy water if you don't mind that we might try and keep any other spirits from trying to attack you during the night and I would like to do that to all who are currently in the room and I might one day include everyone at the villa and maybe those that are currently working on the castle if it seems needed." Father Millinus said with a clear look of intent upon his face holding out the two bottles of holy anointing oil.

I replied, "Sure! What can it hurt? I mean, all I remember was this really odd dream with me and Nathisa and then it seemed everything went black." Father Millinus stated, "Well then, no time to waste! Princess Nathisa, your image is apparently being used by some form of black magic to confuse and trick Sahnedra into lowering her spiritual guard and by these means the spirit being is attacking and trying to drain the life force out of her. So I would like to anoint you first, okay?"

"It would be my honor, Father. Bless me all you can because I don't want to die either." Nathisa said while leaping towards Father Millinus. So Father Millinus blessed Nathisa and then Catherine, Elia and Miranda. Then he proceeded to bless King Dargon, Princess Sahnedra as well as Myra and Vilian. He then grabbed Mercia and blessed her and himself and all the guards that were in attendance.

"Well, by the grace of God that should do it." Father Millinus said with a smile. Nathisa held her stomach and said, "Well, I hope that is all we have to do because my neck feels like it is on fire and my stomach seems to be cramping from something I must have eaten earlier today."

"Well, let me see if I can have Sister Amanda whip up something for you that might settle your stomach and help you with that sunburn issue." Father Millinus said while rummaging through his small bag that he had carried the anointed items in.

"No, Father. I think it will pass. It might just be from all of the excitement of the day and probably mostly because I was so afraid of losing my friends and family from this whatever thing that keeps plaguing us. It seems worse than the black plague at least to me." Nathisa said while holding her stomach.

"Well, princess, you do what you feel is best but if you change your mind, then tell me and I will gladly talk to Sister Amanda." Father Millinus said while picking up his small bag and turning to walk away. "Thank you Father. I will if it gets worse, but this happens once in a while when I get worried or depressed." Nathisa said with a wink in her eye.

As Father Millinus and the others had left, they all began to leave the room to get ready to eat a late supper because no one had eaten all day due to a requested fast for the sake of my return to the kingdom of light that was pleaded for by Father Millinus and King Dargon.

Everyone in the villa was famished and exhausted from the day's events, so all were in a hurry to sit down and thank God for His miracle working power and for allowing them to feast to the safe outcome of my harrowing event.

"So young sister, tell me, what happened last night? I'm all concerned! I heard you had a weird dream about me and this has me so worried because I fear evil is trying to use my image against you because we are so close." Nathisa spoke. "Well Nathisa, the dream was so odd and it really made me feel weird and uncomfortable. You had snuck into my room because in the dream, you stated that your room had issues with the roof leaking and your bed, floor, rugs and clothing were soaked from the day's rain. Does any of this ring true with you?" I questioned. "No Sahnedra. I was in my room all night and my room is as dry as any other room in the villa so I would have had no need to come to your room and sleep with you or share your bed. As a matter of fact, Myra woke me up from my own deep sleep today to tell me that it was difficult for you to wake up. And besides, you exhausted me after you and I went for that long horse ride the other day. By the way, I really enjoyed it and hope we can go out and pick more flowers and see what else lies around the villa to the east. But no, I was out like a candle last night right after we left each other in the washroom. I was ready for a good night's rest." Nathisa said while she nervously glanced around the room.

"Well, also in this dream, you came to me and started to kiss me all over my neck, face and lips. I had this overcoming joy come over me and I started to orally make love to you. And what is so odd is that I couldn't tell if it was real or a dream. It seemed like it was you. It had seemed you wanted to own me and dominate me and make me one with you. What does all this mean? Am I going insane? Am I evil and doing that which is bringing judgment upon my dear Father? Did I somehow cause the death of my Mother and so many others? I can't really say. I enjoyed the experience, but yet it was abhorrent to me as well because you are my best friend outside of my family and the court and I in no way would want to hurt you or do anything wrong to you in any way. Do you believe me?" I asked with tears streaming down my face.

"No, no, my little sister and dear friend. I don't hold you accountable for a dream. Besides, what you dream isn't really you any more than what I dream isn't really me. We both know that evil is always trying to get into our lives and our heads but we must look at it as just that. An evil thought that might have come to us by even something as small as a piece of meat of which we had eaten earlier that day or even a week before. These things are the things of the spirit world and that of the great beyond which is far more than any mere mortal could understand and besides, do you remember that I told you that I was going to reward you? I didn't say that I would harm you but reward you and I would give you the secret to life eternal? Not a life that leads to death but life that can go on for years without end. I would never do anything that would harm you or make you feel wrong. I seek to make our love a good thing and a thing that will last the test of time. Like the love of a true family. One that has no secrets to hide from each other. No pretenses and no lies or misgivings. A love that is truly rare in this world. A love that can transcend the bonds of time as we know it and you my dear can truly receive this gift if you want it. And how do I know this? Well, because you came back to me and wanted more of life and that is what I plan to give you if you want it my dear Sahnedra."

"As a matter of fact, I promise if you will give yourself to me and not hold back anything or any way, then I can promise you that I will protect your kingdom soon with a secret power that will stop all these attacks that have been plaguing your kingdom as of late. Wouldn't you like that?" Nathisa stated while gazing straight into my eyes. "I don't understand all that you have said, but yes, I will do anything for my family and my people. Please, if you can in some way Nathisa, then please protect my father and my family and Father Millinus and all of the others that I love from whatever is happening to us as of late." I said as I drew closer to Nathisa sharing her gaze.

"But how can you a woman stop all of these attacks and things that don't share our normal world with us? And none but God or Satan can give life that doesn't end because one must sell themselves to one or the other to receive one's final judgment. If you believe in Christ, then you receive eternal life. But if not, then one is damned to the fallen kingdom of Satan. But tell me, Nathisa, what do you know of eternal things and how can you stop all of these attacks upon us? Please share this with me and I will go with you anywhere your Father would send you and I will be like your ambassador for my kingdom to any other kingdom you will go. Please help us." I said speaking in a very soft tone while resting my head upon Nathisa's bosom.

"So you *will* be mine? Will you be my best friend in all ways and will give yourself to me willingly and hold nothing back? You promise to not lie to me and will always be at my beckon call and I at yours? Will you share yourself with me in all ways and trust me when I tell you all things? Will you also open your heart to me and be your sister as close as Myra and Vilian? If yes, then after we eat later tonight, then I will tell you everything your heart desires and Sahnedra, if you say amen, then there's no backing out of it because you will have given me your eternal oath.

So I will give you until later tonight after supper to consider your final answer, so be sure and note I can do as I've said and protect your family from all of these attacks and I can stop anyone from taking and harming anyone else in your entire kingdom that is to say from all of these supernatural attacks. Normal everyday life will continue to occur because as you know, life is as life is and God has a plan and a will and no one can stop that but as far as all the things that have been plaguing your kingdom as of late, yes, that I can stop and will if you agree to join me in my travels and be my companion for the rest of our years. So consider what you are about to do and say because once spoken, it is an oath before us forever and cannot be broken and you will be given knowledge of which is powerful and leads to secrets that is hard for the mortal mind to fathom." Nathisa explained as she held me close and kissed the top of my head a few times.

I redirected my gaze up towards Nathisa's eyes, "If you can do that, I will go anywhere and be with you forever but I hope one day to marry and have children, don't you?" Nathisa replied, "One day maybe, but I would like to see what the world has for us first. So let us not talk of this anymore but let us get dressed and go and join the feast that has been prepared for us and remember it is all in your honor. Please enjoy it and spend time with your family because we never know when it will be our last night on this earth as we are and you and I never know what tomorrow will hold for us. But for now, let us eat, drink and be merry in heart and in word." Smiling and leaping up and swaying as if to music, Nathisa held up her hands, winked and spun out of the room leaving one arm still slightly in the doorway with a finger pointing to me and waving me to follow her down to the banquet room for the feast that was made by the court servants to celebrate my miraculous recovery.

So I arose and followed Nathisa after she had finished getting fully dressed and then we walked down the hallway together talking and laughing about the times we had spent together and all that had befallen us over the last little while. We talked no more about what Nathisa had spoken to me about on the bed because Nathisa refused to elaborate upon it until after we had celebrated my joyful miracle.

Dargon raised a glass and began to speak, "I would like to thank God, Father Millinus, the Order of Palin and to you Sister Amanda and the White Order for your service and prayers for my daughter's healing. It would appear that God holds you all in high favor and with that, I say thank you for all you have done for my kingdom over the years. May God bless you and keep you all in the coming days and years and may He add to your works a thousand fold for what you have done for me and my family today. And on a personal note, I would like to say to all of my kingdom, thank you for taking the time to join us in today's requested feast for my daughter's miracle awakening. Without you all, I do not know if she would still be with us right here right now." "Amen!" Father Millinus exclaimed with his glass raised in the air touching King Dargon's as if to bless it yet again.

Sister Amanda rose and started to speak to me as the court gathered at the feast, "Sahnedra, please, our princess in waiting, will you not testify to the goodness of God's great miracle and His saving power and grace? Please encourage the sisters here with us today and tell them how He has done such a great thing for you and if He told you any such things of wisdom while you were in your deep sleep today." And the entire court shouted, "Speak! Speak! Tell us God's words, Sahnedra. Speak!"

I rose up from my chair and slowly bowed my head and raised my glass taking a small sip and began to tell the court what was upon my heart and deep thoughts, "I truly do see the work of God in our kingdom and I feel we are all being tested deeply and severely over the last year. I don't know why or for what purpose, but God has a reason for everything and He will let us all know what His hand is in the affairs of the world when it is His timing. No, I'm sad to say that God didn't impart to me any secret words or wisdom or any great revelation, but what I did see was a vast and great darkness. I feel we are facing down a great evil and we are being entrusted to defeating it and will be given the means to save not only our kingdom, but the entirety of this whole world."

I continued while pausing but for a moment to take another sip of honey wine. "I know that I will do my part and play any role that I must to protect my family, this great court and my dearly beloved kingdom." The court then erupted with shouts and cheers. I gently curtsied while blushing and then continued speaking after it quieted down. "Here me now, my people. I am but a young woman and cannot do it all alone, but with your help, support and prayers; we can and will overcome all that assaults as a kingdom, people and family.

I gratefully thank you for your prayers and for all the candles that were lit for me today and for all that you as a people have done. It was your prayers that got the attention of the archangel Michael and it must have been he that awoke me from a deep sleep and that must have held me close to the door of death itself. I can't and don't have the words to say it enough, but thank you. Thank you all and I love you and will pray for all our kingdom's families that this darkness will be over soon enough." With that, I raised my glass of honey wine and poured it upon the ground and stated, "This is my offering to you, my people. Today, I give up a glass of fine honey wine because today you gave up your time and labor to pray for me and my family. God bless you my people and God bless the King and kingdom forever."

With that, the people that gathered in the room leapt up, rose up and began to pour out wine all around them and shouted, "Sahnedra! Sahnedra! Sahnedra! We love you! You are ours and we are yours!" While this continued, King Dargon rose up and embraced me and hugged and kissed me on my head and had looked into my eyes and said, "This is what I've been waiting for. My little girl has now become a woman that is ready to be a queen. I'm so proud of you and have never been prouder to be called your Father. Can you hear it? They are receiving you as they would have your Mother. You have her gift to deliver a fine and powerful speech. I love you and am so proud of you." Father Millinus then begins to rise and compliments, "Amen! Fine speech, my girl. Fine, fine speech. I knew you weren't always ignoring me when we were talking about talking from your heart and not just from your head. That was such a good speech. I've never had up to this time such a good student since I taught your Mother years back when she first married your father all those many years ago. You will be a great queen one day just like your Mother. She would be so proud and I'm sure she is watching you now from heaven. I could have sworn she was speaking through you a few minutes ago. Wonderful job, my girl. Wonderful job." Father Millinus stated while gently patting my left hand and then he returned to his seat.

The court was still vibrant with voices and songs began to break out while Nathisa reached over and grabbed me by the hand and said, "What a great speech. You are a powerful speaker and what a princess! Someday soon, my queen, you will be for a greater people than this." With a pull to her heart and a kiss on the hand, Nathisa let my hand go so who was still standing could allow me to wave at all the people who by now were still chanting my name and a few had broke into Satu Mare's anthem with all the men at arms and the court standing in attention. And yet, others who were a little more loaded up with harder wine were throwing coins up to the table beside the court so as to help with the cost of the candles that had been purchased by the poorer of the kingdom for the sake of the princess's healing prayers towards Michael the archangel. And the rest would be gathered up and put in the fund towards the cost of rebuilding of the Order of Palin's building cost and the needs of the poor.

After a long night of talking, drinking and speeches, things finally began to wind down and the court began to clear out about 10:30 pm. Nathisa, myself as well as all our friends began to rise up and walk together to their rooms and one by one hugged and kissed each other goodnight and they all told me they were thankful that I was brought back to them by the archangel Michael and that they were happily awaiting tomorrow and their trip to the market for foods, spices and clothing and other such exciting things as they could think of to buy and bring back to the villa because it had been such a long time since many of them had been back to Satu Mare proper.

So Nathisa and I were the last to make it to our assigned rooms and were busy talking about the night's events when Nathisa began to speak, "Do you remember what we had talked about earlier tonight?" "Yes," I stated with a whimsical look on my face. "Well, if you have decided, then please let me know and I will come to your room and tell you all you want to know or need to have answered about what we discussed today. But remember, once you agree, it is your word and your oath to me before yourself, I and God, okay?" Nathisa said while glancing down the hallway with my hand in hers.

"Okay, you heard what I said at the feast tonight. I will do anything I must to save and protect everyone I care about and that includes you Nathisa. So yes, I agree. I will go with you and do what we need to do to protect our kingdoms and our loved ones as well as ourselves. So what is all this you must tell me?" I asked in a rather incredulous tone.

"Okay. Then let's rush over to your room and there I will tell you what I know and how we can make it all go away," Nathisa said while rushing over to my door and opening it to see if anyone else was in the room or not.

"So here is what I want to tell you and remember, you and I swore to never lie to each other nor to keep any secrets from one another ever. So I being true to my word am giving you the secret truth to all that is taking place here and now and then you as agreed must give yourself to me if you want it all to stop and if you don't give yourself to me and you break your promise, then I can tell you hell will break out all over the countryside and I will not be able to protect your kingdom from the powers that will come." Nathisa expressed while standing at the window with a look of worry on her face. "Are you threatening me and my kingdom with war?" I questioned while standing beside Nathisa. "No, but I do know about things that are coming and about things that would like nothing better than to consume this whole part of the world and to create a small kingdom right here and right now. You gave me your word just a few minutes ago out in the hallway. Don't make me regret trusting you because the cost could be high for the both of us." Nathisa said while gazing into my eyes. "Then be on with it! Tell me all that is happening and then I can tell Father and he can rally his army and with the Russian army standing by our sides, nothing can stop us." I said while turning away from Nathisa.

"No silly. That isn't going to happen. Russia has nothing to do with this nor does any other earthly power. But an eternal power is at hand. A power that reaches back since the fall of mankind. A power that can make light dark and dark light. Can we sit down on the bed please so I can speak plainly?" Nathisa asked. I acquiesced to Nathisa's question and we both sat down and Nathisa began to speak and she stated, "I'm going to be plain with you as I said,"

Suddenly, there was a knock on the door. "Is everything okay, Princess?" Stimer asked. "Yes, Stimer, thank you. Everything is fine. Nathisa and I are talking right now and enjoying each other's company before we head off to bed. Good night!" I said being somewhat annoyed at the interruption. "Well, good night Princess Sahnedra and as well to you Princess Nathisa." And then he walked briskly away.

"Okay, let's try this again. I'm not just a Russian princess, but a princess as you will soon be of a far older order called the kingdom. Their goal is to one day run the world in secret from behind the scenes and you are now introduced into this order. This order is of a vampiress kingdom that has been around since the dawn of man right after the fall. It began with the line of Cain and continued through the flood of Noah." I interrupted, "How can that be? The Great Flood killed everyone." "Not true," Nathisa continued almost not missing a beat of her past statement. "The Flood killed mortal man and many if not most of the hybrids of the sons of God, but a few of the sturdy ones managed to survive all the way to the drying of the waters by various means that the ancients have kept secret to themselves until this day.

I myself am a princess and you will be as well and who knows? Maybe one day we will be high kingdom queens of one of the twelve vampiress provinces each of which is ruled by a vampiress, prince or king. All this depends upon their age and wisdom as well as have they been killed or not broken one of the vampiress laws." "Alright! I've had about enough of this! You are just trying to scare me and it's not funny anymore! You claim to be my friend and I almost died the other night having a horrific dream of you and me and...wait a minute...it *was* you!! You did come into my room and you bit me! That's what vampires do, don't they? They bite people! They drink their blood and eat their flesh or something and turn them into slaves of darkness," I said with a fearful look on my face with a raised voice.

"No, my little sister. You only have it half right. You gave me your word and I'm keeping mine and you will now keep yours. I have much more to tell you, but let's set the record straight. We are not bats, but we can fly or change shape if we want to. We don't eat flesh but we do drink blood but not all the time. We can go for years if we so choose before we feed again, but that takes practice and as with anything, one learns to control their powers with the passage of the years.

Please sit back down! You gave yourself to me and there is now nothing no one can do for you and we are going to go through with our agreement tonight." I continued to back up and said, "I could scream and run away and you might not find me. The villa's guards could be in here in minutes and maybe kill you." "Well, if you want to try it, then be my guest because I'm very fast and I could just kill you instead of making you immortal. I would hate to kill off any more of your guards and those sisters do look tasty. And your Father? Wow! I would love to share his bed for a night and prolong his turning or maybe just kill him after I'm done with him. What do you think I should do after you break your oath to me?" Nathisa said glaring and then with a swift movement cut my pathway to the door.

"Please leave my family out of this! Don't bother my sisters or my Father! Don't hurt anyone! Please!" I cried while Nathisa grabbed me by the throat and licked playfully at my neck. "Oh, I don't plan on it unless you make me and I always keep my word to whoever I make it. You see, that is one of the laws of the vampiress kingdom. If you make a promise to a mortal, then you must keep it because if you don't, then the kingdom will send its enforcers after you until you keep your word. And if you can't, then God might send an angel after you and smite you and release you from their pledge of service to you. And I wouldn't want to lose you. Not after all this time of developing such a good and close relationship. I do love you and view you as a sister and a beloved friend."

"But why me and why my kingdom and family? Did you kill my mother?" I questioned falling to the floor and my face drowning with tears. "First off, I chose this kingdom because it used to belong to my family during the days of the Roman Empire. Not all of it, but a good large part of it back before my turning. Your family means little to me except that they are important to you so they have become important to me as well. And as far as your mother goes, no, that was most unfortunate. The one that caused all that trouble which by the way was totally unplanned for was Ralisu, the young soldier that was bitten right before I came here." Nathisa stated while bending down on her knee caressing my head.

"Don't blame Ralisu. He couldn't control himself. He has as yet to be able to fully control his powers of rage and changing form. Most of the time, they learn to control their form within three years after their turning, but some do so a little earlier than that and others never can. The ones that never learn to discipline themselves end up dead by men hunting them down or we do because we can't afford to let our secret get out among the mortals. And your Father? Wow! I would love to share his bed for a night and prolong his turning or maybe just kill him after I'm done with him. What do you think I should do after you break your oath to me?" Nathisa said glaring and then with a swift movement cut my pathway to the door.

With a kiss upon my head, Nathisa continued, "Sahnedra, he is now an immortal as you will soon become." Trying to push Nathisa back away from me, I began to speak, "Why is he what you are and what you seek to make me? You said you were my friend and wouldn't hurt me. Why me? What did I do to you? I don't want to die! Please don't kill me!" Nathisa laughs, "Okay, so your word means nothing then and I should set about killing everyone in this place. I can do that. But I think you are just afraid of the unknown because you don't yet understand. I'm not killing you but lifting you up to eternal life such as not been in the lives of daily man since the fall of Adam. The mark of God that was placed upon Cain was upon his neck and then God made Cain desire the blood of mankind for all eternity since he slew his brother Abel and because Abel's blood cried out to God from the ground then did God curse Cain with an unquenchable desire for blood until one day he was killed by a human being or he broke another law of truth by breaking his word to a mortal man. At that point, then God would send an avenging angel out after Cain to punish him and to destroy his immortal soul and body once and for all. But that is not what you need to know for now and is a story for you in another time and place of my choosing when I teach you about the full history of the vampires.

Now as to Ralisu, no, that poor soul isn't what I am. He is a Lycan and they are our servant army of avengers and our force that terrifies and does some of our bidding. We have vampire armies of course to keep everything in line and then there are the enforcers that enforce the vampiress laws so we don't run up against breaking our own codes of ethics as it were. But as to why you, my dear, well, it's because when I saw you after your Father and his men killed four of our scouts, well, from that moment, I knew I needed the blood from a family member of such a man. Be it a man or a woman, I didn't honestly care at the time but I knew that I wanted one of the family members to be a part of our kingdom because it takes such bravery and skill to kill not one but four of our Lycans which is a testament to the power of bravery of such a family and kingdom.

I chose this kingdom because I found you worthy of me and my kind. I knew since the moment I first spied you out of my carriage that I wanted you and I couldn't wait to taste you. Besides, who do you think it was that sent out a beast man as you called it to find you and protect you from your attacker in the woods? I couldn't allow anything to happen to my sister and I would not allow him to defile you in any way. Your defender was none other than Ralisu who slipped past his keepers at the time and went out at my mental command to find you and keep watch on you. He was to keep you safe and sound at all cost until you were mine.

I can see it in your eyes. Why did I send Ralisu and force him to use his powers? Well, because he knew your scent and I couldn't afford to send out one of my Lycan warriors that are with me even now in the castle at that time and the villa now. Yes, Sahnedra, my escorts are all Lycans both the men and the women, but you and your people have nothing to fear because they have shown us kindness. We will do them no harm and not one of my Lycans have attacked nor harmed any of your people. You are probably wondering who killed the Queen and her guards. Well, that again was Ralisu and as I stated, that was a totally unintended mishap because when I forced him to transform outside of the castle to look for you when you had been late returning home from your joy ride, I did it to him during the daylight hours because of my fear that harm might befall. I tasted you before any man and in all ways that makes us bonded together as sisters and more. So forgive me, but I think the loss of your mother was worth me sparing your entire kingdom the horrors my friends and I could bring upon it, don't you?"

By now, I had run to my bed and grabbed a pillow and cowered in a corner hugging it tight just staring silently at Nathisa. "So you are going to kill me and drink my blood all the while you mock me and threaten my family?? You're a monster! I hate you! Stay away from me! Please do anything you want, but don't kill me or any of my people!" I howled out.

"I'm really sorry little sister, but that's not how this works. I told you earlier tonight that if you agreed to give yourself over to me that it was a blood oath and couldn't be altered now or ever. "No you didn't," I responded, "you also said that you wouldn't hurt me and besides, you never said that you would make me a blood-drunk fiend! I could barely handle a glass of wine at the festival let alone stand the sight of blood. I almost passed out viewing my bloody sheets today after I woke up and now you are going to kill me?! Please let me live! Please don't hurt me!" Nathisa smiles and with a thought glides in closer to me as to which my eyes are affixed upon her wide open and horrified. "Now little sister, I can let you go and forget all about this offer of eternal life but I will have to allow my people to kill hundreds perhaps thousands more of your people because you would have broken your word. I would hate to do that, but I will give you a choice once more than I ever had and besides I have now given you three different times to choose to accept me or reject me and I truly do tire of this game quickly. But as I said, your choice. But be careful because I might have to try one of your sisters and I'm leaning towards baby Vilian. Let's see...what *is* she, fifteen now? Yes, such a sweet fine age to make immortal. She could do such wonderful things with her powers especially being chosen at such a young, healthy age. Wow! Maybe you're right. Maybe you aren't worthy of me and maybe I should choose Vilian. She might accept me a lot easier. The young are so much more ready to believe anything one tells them."

Nathisa brushed my hair back and gave my neck a soft kiss.

"Wait!" I screamed. "What are you doing? I'm not ready yet! Please! I need to pray first before you kill me!" Nathisa laughed and with a smile stated, "Dear sister, I'm done. I'm not going to kill you. I'm showing you my love for you. I'm going to let you live out the rest of your days in a normal human life. I'm setting about to wipe your memory of this and the last few days' events. Don't say that I've not been more than fair because I need someone else who truly loves me as I love them and you don't know what it means to be honest with me." "No, please wait! Don't hurt Vilian! She's so young or any of my family! You promise if I allow you to have me without any rules that you will leave my people alone, safe and unharmed from this night forward?" Nathisa swiftly nodded, "Yes, sister, I do, but I ask you for the last time. Can I have all of you? And you will now or never hold back anything from me at the penalty of vengeance?" "What does penalty of vengeance mean?" I questioned.

"Well, it means if you lie to me, then I will kill your family one by one in front of your very eyes while the enforcers make you watch and then I might kill you if you've angered me enough at the time." Nathisa said with a sound of irritation in her voice. "So let's get on with this, shall we? I don't have all night."

I immediately fell down at Nathisa's feet with tears streaming down my face and began to pray, "Oh God, forgive me and please don't let my sin be held against me forever. Remember her words and protect my family and my soul from evil. Forgive me Daddy and Mommy. Please turn away while this takes place. Oh, God, protect

Daddy and my two sisters and please don't let Father Millinus think ill of me, Amen."

With that, Nathisa grabbed me forcefully by the hands and picked me up and threw me down on the bed and said, "You're all mine now!"

I just laid on the bed with my eyes closed begging Nathisa to get it over and done with. I also prayed silently that God would end this torment as soon as possible. Nathisa reading my thoughts quickly turned back towards my face and smacked me and said, "Little sister, you are mine now and forever and you will be mine until I let you loose." She grabbed the back of my head and held it forcefully with her hands clenched in my hair while staring into my tear-drenched face. It was almost as if I could read what she was thinking as I was staring back at her. Within seconds, she dug her now appearing fangs into my neck. I winced miserably in pain and began to try to resist as I could feel the life rushing out of my body. It was literally draining from me and my heart began to race faster and faster almost in a rhythmic nature with Nathisa's. At this point, she was close to finishing the deed of bringing me over.

Suddenly, she removed her hand from the back of my head and laid it down on the pillow and said quietly, "I will see you in seventy-two hours, my beloved sister. Your senses will develop over the next three full days and nights and after which I will be there to get you. I'm so sorry. I'm sorry if I hurt you more than I had to. I just sometimes cannot control the feeding rage. Please forgive me. I do love you and we are family. I don't want to hurt you anymore." With a still small whisper, I responded to her, "Remember your promise. Please. Remember no harm to my family or people. I...I forgive you Nathisa…" and with that, I drifted off quietly into the night.

Nathisa looking down in horror as to what she had done to me comes close to my ear and says, "Your body is dying and that is why you are winching and jerking, but your ears still are working and can always hear what is going on around you from this point forward. I will leave your people in peace and you have fed me tonight. Now, drink of me my sister and come see me in the next few days." With that, Nathisa takes a finger and cuts her wrist and places it gently to my mouth so her blood could flow inside of me. Then she laid herself back on the bed and proceeded to pierce her body with a knife and also her neck until blood comes gushing out of her as well.

The next morning, the guards are abuzz with excitement. They believe I am dead and Nathisa is barely alive. The King is in fits and the whole court is in chaos. Everyone is wondering how this could have happened within a day of each other.

With Trist gone on a journey to Rome, the duties of Commander of the Army falls to Drang and he sets about to find out who has done this and how the person or persons could have gotten past the full guard. But that is a story for another time.

Sister Amanda tended to Princess Nathisa's wounds and placed salve upon her body to help keep the infection down. She and the White Order were also assigned the grim task of preparing my body for burial.

The whole kingdom is in a state of shock and horror and many of the people came to the villa and offered presents to my Father and the family. The state funeral was to be held on the following day giving time for Princess Nathisa to recover enough that she might be able to attend her best friend's funeral. The procession was as the last almost to a point with few changes. The queen's guard became the princess's guard and they were followed by orphans that lived at the villa with the Sisters of the White Order. They threw out fruit and seeds to the people who were in lines in places twenty deep along the roadways and paths all the way to Satu Mare's royal graveyard. The children all wore white and sang songs of love for me and held candles that constantly needed to be relit along the way in hopes of summoning Raphael to come and guide my vexed spirit home to heaven to be with my mother Vinician who was believed to be waiting for me at the gates with Saint Peter. Following the children and the sisters was the whole of the royal court. So many of the court attended my funeral that the villa had not one soul left in it until they all returned from the funeral procession. After the royals of the court and the servants that followed after them came, Princess Nathisa who was riding atop her royal carriage was visibly shaken and bruised and cut and in places still wearing blood through bandages. She was waved at by the people and well wishers ran up to her carriage and touched it as she slowly but tearfully passed by them. Following after that was a contingent of the king's royal guard which were dressed in full battle gear and formation all riding with each royal flag in their hands. As they passed, the people who watched them pass them on their battle horse who also was decked out in full battle attire. Following them were my Father and his two remaining daughters all of whom were wearing the darkest black and wearing clothing of common people. My sisters were crying uncontrollably and King Dargon was just sitting on top of the royal carriage staring into space. Just wringing his hands and staying unmoved and quiet. Following the king was Father Millinus and the entire Order of Palin who had stopped all work on the Order's buildings upon hearing the news of the attack upon both princesses. But now the Order of Palin was in battle gear both spiritual and physical. Father Millinus had ordered the Order to fetch its weapons to bless them and from this point forward be ready to attack any force that comes near the castle with evil intent. Father Millinus also had sent priests ahead in full battle gear to prepare the grave site for the arrival of my remains. He had some bless the grave while others set up watch for anything that might seek to harm the remaining royal family. As far as Father Millinus was concerned, it was now a war he prayed he could win.

As the procession arrived at the royal graveyard, throngs of people followed in behind the tail of the Order of Palin. I wasn't just a princess to the people, but I was their princess. Many of the people had rejoiced at my birth and now many more people from the young to the old were there to share the family's sorrow at my death and all wanted to hear the words of comfort and wisdom of Father Millinus who was himself having a hard time holding back his tears and keeping his composure at the loss of a child he often called his own. And in his mind, he often imagined if he had chosen to have a family that God might have given him a daughter such as me. At these mere thoughts, he broke out in tears as the casket was lowered down before the people to a resting place before it was placed into its final resting place in the ground.

A group of four young priests came forward and slowly opened the casket that held my body. As the priests finished fully opening the casket, a hush came upon the whole crowd that was gathered. Following the King was Father Millinus and the entire Order of Palin who had stopped all work on the Orders buildings upon hearing the news of the attack upon both princesses. But now the Order of Palin was in battle gear both spiritual and physical. Father Millinus had ordered the Order to fetch its weapons to bless them and from this point forward be ready to attack any force that comes near the castle with evil intent. Father Millinus also had sent the priest ahead in full battle gear to prepare the grave site for the arrival of Princess Sahnedra's remains. He had some bless the grave while others set up watch for anything that might seek to harm the remaining royal family. As far as Father Millinus was concerned, it was now a war he prayed he could win.

As the procession arrived at the royal graveyard, throngs of people followed in behind the tail of the Order of Palin. I wasn't just a princess to the people, but I was their princess. Many of the people had rejoiced at my birth and now many more people from the young to the old were there to share the family's sorrow at my death and all wanted to hear the words of comfort and wisdom of Father Millinus who was himself having a hard time holding back his tears and keeping his composure at the loss of a child he often called his own. And in his mind, he often imagined if he had chosen to have a family that God might have given him a daughter such as me. At these mere thoughts, he broke out in tears as the casket was lowered down before the people to a resting place before it was placed into its final resting place in the ground.

A group of four young priests came forward and slowly opened the casket that held my body. As the priests finished fully opening the casket, a hush came upon the whole crowd that was gathered. People could not believe that I was dead and tears, screams, howls and crying could be heard throughout the crowd. The king was a mess and the sisters each passed out at the sight of their beloved sister lying there motionless, lifeless and cold to the touch. Father Millinus sat down and beckoned a younger priest to begin to speak for him until he could gain his strength back after seeing such a sight.

The young priest began to speak when Father Millinus arose and said, "My young brother, forgive me, but I owe this to my beloved princess and to my king and his people. Please pray for me that God gives me the strength to continue through this ultimate test." Father Millinus couldn't hold back the tears as he ascended to the pulpit that was hastily set up so the good Father could address those that were gathered. The young priest bowed and handed God's Holy Word to the Father and silently moved back to where the other priests and sisters were standing. Father Millinus addressed the crowd while tears continued to stream down his cheeks, "We are gathered here today to do what is to me the hardest of my sacred duties to this kingdom. I have helped birth many among you and ordained many to God and His Church. Even more of you I have baptized and been there at various times of need, but this my people is the hardest thing I've ever had to do. My King and my personal friend today sits in shock, almost unable to move as he watches me say the final words over his dearly departed daughter. What makes this even harder is the fact that he was here not too many months ago when we buried our dear Queen Vinician. But today, Sahnedra was called home after a vicious attack that had taken place in the villa. This attack took place while our guards kept watch and no one saw nor heard anything. Dear Princess Nathisa was also attacked, but fortunately lived through the horrific event. She as well as Sahnedra were violated while we all slept just minutes away from them. How this happened and who did it we none know at this time, but I want this kingdom to rest assured that the Order of Palin is searching out this evil and studying every book we have and when we find out who or what is attacking our kingdom, then we will set about to kill it. God says vengeance is His, but I say in this matter I believe He will leave it in the hands of God's servants. I cannot rest until I find my girl's killer. Sahnedra was a friend of mine. A child I helped to raise and educate. She was a student of mine and I will surely miss her. It is a hard thing for anyone to lose a family member, but when one outlives your child, well, that is even a worse pain because you had children to raise up grandchildren to one's self." A younger priest came up and patted Father Millinus on the back and handed him a cup of water. He swallows the water and handed the empty cup back to the young priest and continued on, "My heart aches today, but I truly believe that God recalled Michael back to heaven so he could allow Sahnedra to come to him. I believe that all things work together for the good of them that love God and I believe this includes all the losses we in this kingdom have faced. Because as Job says, "The Lord gives and He takes away, but at the end of Job's trying, God gave him two times the amount of items and children that he had lasted so in the end, Job had more both in material wealth as well as in a spiritual heritage then he had in the beginning. When he finally arrived in heaven to meet his God, then he didn't just have seven children, but he had fourteen. And I don't know how or why, but I believe that God is also going to give King Dargon the same as He gave Job two times as much as he had at the start of these trials and testings. So bow with me right now in a brief moment of personal prayer and pray for this kingdom, God's Church and your King and the family. Pray with us to yourself and help us overcome this darkness together in the name of the Lord and His Son Jesus Christ and His Holy Spirit, Amen. Let us pray." A few minutes later, Father Millinus said amen again and the people began to slowly disperse after each passed by the casket where I now laid.

After the crowd and family all had passed by and given their final respects to me, Father Millinus waved at the priests and grave men around as they slowly closed the lid of the casket. While the family and court cried, they slowly lowered me into the cold earth on that day. As the grave men began to cover my casket over with dirt, the day began to slowly turn from a warming day to yet another colder rainy day. The storm clouds began to rush in and the wind began to whip things around violently and all the men and priests who were around rushed to finish the finishing touch on burying me. Finally, Father Millinus placed a cross over the top of the grave as a precaution so that I would not become a servant of the undead. This was done because they still had very little clues as to what took place during the attack of myself and Nathisa and no one knew how anyone or anything could get past the guards, dogs and priests as well as everyone else that was in the villa that night without one person being alerted. But this time, Father Millinus took no chances and blessed the ground and each grave at the site in an attempt to conquer the evil that had attacked the kingdom and the royal family.

As day became night as it always does, time went from one day to the next. No one had gotten relief by burying me and in fact, security was tightened to where the sisters were told to wear knives so as they might protect themselves from an attack and perhaps help protect the children if the attacker perhaps snuck past the guards and dogs again.

The king ordered nightly patrols by armed horsemen from that day forward for each of his cities that were under his protection and he called up all the army and even the reserves and ordered that forts be built along the roadways of the kingdoms to ensure safety for trade and the people.

But as day two passed, no one noticed anything different but then came day three. It was cold and wet because it seemed as if since my funeral that the heavens had joined the kingdom of Satu Mare in crying for me and that I had been taken from this earth before my time. But that night, on the seventy-second hour of my attack, life began to spring back into my body. I began to twitch and then shake violently. I tried to rise up, but hit my head against some wooden lid. As the air rushed back into my lungs, all I could see was complete darkness. I began to frantically feel around and cried, "Oh no! I'm in a coffin! I went from my bed to a casket! I'm trapped! Oh God, help me! I'm so hungry! I feel like I haven't eaten in years! God help me! Anyone, get me out of here! I'm alive!" All the while, I struggled, hit, punched and kicked to try and break out of the casket that now entombed me for what I feared would be the rest of my life. "Please! If you can hear me, help me!!" I shouted. But all was still and worse yet, pitch black and dark. The cold, wet ground could be felt all around the casket. I continued to weep uncontrollably. I didn't want to end up dying like this. I felt as if my lungs started to collapse. Holding my chest, I cried out for one last time, "Won't you help me? Please! I'm trapped!" Then suddenly, all of the air had exhausted from my lungs and I immediately and fearfully began to see utter darkness. In those brief moments, the world had begun to become silent and I was literally all alone.

Printed in the United States
By Bookmasters